THE ASSASSINS

A Clint Smith Thriller

Bob Doerr

TotalRecall Publications, Inc.
1103 Middlecreek
Friendswood, Texas 77546
281-992-3131   281-482-5390 Fax
www.mousegate.com

Copyright © 2018 by: Bob Doerr
All rights reserved
ISBN: 978-1-59095-196-5
UPC: 6-43977-41964-4

Library of Congress Control Number:

Printed in the United States of America with simultaneous printings in Australia, Canada, and United Kingdom.

FIRST EDITION
1   2   3   4   5   6   7   8   9   10

To those who serve.

Award Winning Author: Bob Doerr

 grew up in a military family, graduated from the Air Force Academy, and had a career of his own in the Air Force. Bob specialized in criminal investigations and counter-intelligence gaining significant insight to the worlds of crime, espionage, and terrorism. His work brought him into close coordination with the security agencies of many countries and filled his mind with the fascinating plots and characters found in his books today. His education credits include a Masters in International Relations from Creighton University. A full time author with thirteen published books and a co-author in another, Bob was selected by the Military Writers Society of America as its Author of the Year for 2013. The Eric Hoffer Awards awarded *No One Else to Kill* its 2013 first runner up to the grand prize for commercial fiction. Two of his other books were finalists for the Eric Hoffer Award in earlier contests. *Loose Ends Kill* won the 2011 Silver medal for Fiction/mystery by the Military Writers Society of America. *Another Colorado Kill* received the same Silver medal in 2012 and the silver medal for general fiction at the Branson Stars and Flags national book contest in 2012. Bob has also written three novellas for middle grade readers in the Enchanted Coin series: *The Enchanted Coin, The Rescue of Vincent,* and *The Magic of Vex.* Bob lives in Garden Ridge, Texas, with Leigh, his wife of 45 years, and Cinco, their ornery cat.

About the Book

A disputed election has divided the nation, and a handful of senior government officials have conspired to have the North Koreans assassinate the President of the United States. Believing the assassination attempt to be only days away, Theresa Deer, Director of the Special Section, a small unit whose existence is known by only a few in the U.S. government, is tasked to interdict the man intent on providing the North Koreans vital information about the president's itinerary for his visit to South Korea. While Deer succeeds in her mission, she is severely injured and finds herself being hunted by the North Korean assassins. Clint Smith is sent to Korea to help Deer get back to the U.S. and finds himself caught in a deadly game of cat and mouse with the North Koreans. With no one in the U.S. government to turn to for help, and the South Koreans now also hunting them, getting out of South Korea alive is looking unlikely.

Acknowledgement

"Many people have read my books
and gone on to lead normal lives."

CHAPTER 1

She crouched low against the large trash bin and listened but heard nothing. The light mist that had been falling for a while had finally soaked through her so-called weather resistant pullover making her shiver. She couldn't control the shivering which had gotten worse in the last few minutes, but she managed to resist the gag reflex from the stench. A trash pile twenty yards wide and ten feet high sat only a few yards on the other side of the bin and the dozen or so other nearby trash bins. Rotting food, along with whatever else comprised the mass of goo, produced the most awful odor.

"Stay focused," she murmured to herself. She couldn't hear her pursuers, but she knew they were still out there in the darkness. Low clouds made the night even darker than usual. If her pursuers had night vision equipment they would've already caught and killed her. Their small flashlights did little to cut through the darkness. Twice in the last hour, they had been close enough to almost touch her. The last time was in the rare patch of forest a good thirty minutes ago.

A small animal sprinted by her and away from the pile of garbage. Something had spooked it. She heeded the animal's heads up, and staying low to the ground, she hurried after it. She hoped the animal had the sense to run in a direction away from the threat.

Without warning a man came out of the darkness and slammed into her right side, knocking her off her feet and onto the muddy ground. She managed to keep a grip on the CZ82 pistol in her right hand, but before she could maneuver to fire, the man pounced on top of her and struck a glancing blow with his fist to her head.

Half dazed and with her right arm now pinned, she reacted instinctively and with her left hand rammed all four inches of the Spyderco's blade into the man's side. Her attacker jerked away, and she took advantage of the separation by stabbing him in the solar plexus. She twisted the blade, and her assailant went limp.

She rolled away from him and stood up. A dim light appeared to her right, and she felt the burn of the round ripping across her belly and through her left arm before the soft chirp of the weapon registered in her mind. The impact caused her to let go of the knife. Dropping to one knee, she fired two silenced rounds back toward the light and heard the man grunt and fall. The light disappeared in the mud.

More men were out there somewhere in the dark searching for her. She ran a short distance and stopped by some bushes. Silence. Her pursuers must have split up. Her arm and stomach burned, and she felt a little light headed. Crouching, she took a chance and activated the GPS on her watch. She had two and a half miles to the edge of Pyongtek and then another half mile to her hotel. The rain started to come down harder, and it could be daylight by the time she reached her hotel.

Her original plan had her back in her hotel room by this time. She needed to take the most direct route now, and that meant crossing a large open field. The field offered no place to hide but would save her considerable time. If discovered, she would be a sitting duck. Well perhaps not a sitting duck, but definitely a cold, wet, muddy, tired, bloody, and angry duck.

She reached the open field in less than an hour without encountering any more of her pursuers. For the most part, the pitch-black sky remained her ally, and the occasional headlight of the distant cars did nothing to light up the area around her.

However, the uneven ground took advantage of the darkness by hiding holes and rocks the size of softballs. Despite a need for speed, walking at a slower, steady pace helped her maintain her balance, but even where the ground seemed smooth she encountered mud. Several of her steps caused suction sounds in the mud when she lifted a foot. She hoped her pursuers were nowhere close enough to hear her. A half hour passed before she neared the road.

This last part of her trek should at least work as planned. She buried the small CZ82 handgun in a shallow hole in the mud before walking the last twenty yards to the road. Even if found at some later date, the Czech made weapon was commonly used by the North Koreans, not the Americans.

She took a thin reflective safety vest and head band from her hip pack and put on the vest. Instead of putting the reflective head band on her head, she double wrapped it around the wound on her arm. She took off her thoroughly drenched, black stocking cap and wiped the black camo stripes from her face before putting it back on her head.

She started a slow jog on the old, one lane road that paralleled the newer, adjacent highway into Pyongtek, South Korea. She wasn't far from the large US military base, and she knew soldiers frequently used this road for jogging. Anyone driving by should take her for a dedicated runner, not smart enough to stay inside on this wet morning. The rain turned into a steady downpour thoroughly soaking her, but it also washed a lot of the mud and blood off her. Still, she didn't start to relax until the buildings of the city surrounded her, and the hint of a rising sun appeared behind her.

The drivers of the occasional car or truck that passed her on the adjacent highway did not seem to take any interest in her. Well inside the city, she took a little used side road to her hotel rather than the main street that ran in front of it. She entered the hotel through a back door and took the stairs up three flights to her room. The hotel had elevators and a nicer stairway by the reception desk, but for obvious reasons, Theresa Deer didn't want to use the front entrance.

CHAPTER 2

Deer showered and did her best to clean the wounds to her arm and stomach. The stomach wound where the round had grazed her was not much worse than a deep, wide, long scratch. It wouldn't require stitches, but could possibly leave an ugly scar. The arm, however, needed medical attention. The bullet had passed through the fleshy part of her upper arm leaving a small hole where it entered the arm and a large tear where it left.

"Later," she said to herself.

She started to feel dizzy again and a little lightheaded. After she tied a towel that she had brought with her around her midsection to keep pressure on the wound to her stomach, she wrapped and tied a tee shirt around the wound to her arm using her mouth to help pull the knot tight. After placing a do not disturb sign on the door, Deer pushed the bed away from the wall and lay down on the floor to sleep. She didn't want to leave any blood on the sheets, and while the dark pattern on the carpet might make it hard to see the blood, she also didn't think anyone would look under the bed for a long time.

The last thing Deer thought before she passed out was what a fool she had been to assign this mission to herself.

Three hours later, someone vacuuming outside the hotel room door woke her. She reacted by trying to spring into a sitting position only to gasp in pain and collapse back to the floor. Her head pulsed in pain, and her left arm burned like a hot poker had seared it. She fought to control the panic that invaded her. Taking a few deep breaths, she focused on a spot above her on the ceiling.

"Come on, old girl, you've been in many worse situations

than this," she said aloud.

She sat up, this time using her uninjured arm to push off the floor. She saw the blood stain on the rug. It would have caused a lot of chatter among the hotel staff if she had left the stain on the bed sheets. Today would not be a good day for such gossip. Deer felt sure the bodies would be found, and that the South Korean press would be in a frenzy with the discovery. The discovery of a dead American, and three North Korean agents did not happen every day.

Deer stood up and pushed the bed back against the wall. She inspected her wounds and discovered that the long crease across her stomach had almost stopped bleeding. The wound to her arm hadn't. She wrapped it tightly with a new t shirt. The wound required medical attention, and that wouldn't be easy to do today. She worried about the amount of blood she had already lost.

After brewing a cup of hotel coffee and opening the blinds on the one window in the room, Deer sat down and began to plan how she could extricate herself from this mess.

It had been five days since she had met with Leon Thomas. He had requested the meeting, something he had not done in two years. Thomas filled the senior permanent position on the National Security Advisor's staff. Political appointees came and left, but Thomas had been there since Deer's small agency had been created shortly after 9/11. Deer believed he might be the last person in government who knew what she and her hunters did.

Shortly after World War II, the U.S. government, as the largest employer in the nation, had become too huge to be effectively managed. This vast bureaucracy developed a life of its own. As a result, redundancy and waste had grown, overwhelming the government and ultimately the tax payers. The intelligence community had taken full advantage of this trend. Its size and budget had skyrocketed in the last thirty years. New agencies such as CIA, NSA, and DIA were born with noble ideals but grew into gluttonous, inefficient bureaucracies. At the same time, those at the very top became less aware of what was going on below them. Budgetary battles, personnel issues, and crisis management had become the leadership's top priorities.

Even worse, politicians began to exert their influence over these agencies in an attempt to use them for their party's political power. Following the old axiom that "knowledge is power", these politicians did their best to use the agencies against their political enemies.

The average operator and staffer in all these agencies still worked as hard as always, but leadership's control and management of daily operations had been delegated down so far in the chain that Deer's small office had no trouble operating virtually invisible to the rest of the government. That's not to say her office didn't appear in some government flow chart or budget, but its true mission had remained hidden.

"Glad you could make it, Theresa," Thomas said after she joined him on a bench overlooking the Potomac River.

"It's good to see you again, Leon. What can I do for you?"

"This is one of my favorite spots along the river. I could sit out here all day." Thomas stared at the water and appeared to collect his thoughts.

Deer waited for him to say something. She didn't have to wait long.

"We've got a nasty situation. It's got to be handled quickly and quietly and not allowed to develop." He stopped talking and seemed to focus on the river again.

"Are you okay?" Deer asked.

"Yes," he forced a small smile. "We've got something developing that I thought I'd never see in this country. I hope I'm exaggerating, but we've developed some information that a handful of senior people in our government are conspiring to assassinate the President of the United States."

"What?" Deer asked.

"I know. It sounds crazy. It's not uncommon for this country to nominate and elect individuals from either party who have no business being president, but we've always let the system work."

"What evidence do you have?"

"Very little left alive. Three weeks ago, a retired three-star general contacted the Secret Service and provided a lengthy statement about a plot brewing among some senior government officials and a few retired ones to assassinate the president. It seemed too fantastic to be real, but the Secret Service opened an investigation. Two days later the general disappeared and hasn't been seen since. The one person he identified as being part of the plot has also disappeared."

"That should've sent flares up that something was going on," Deer said.

"Of course. The Secret Service has made this its top priority, and as you might expect, the security around the president is tighter than ever."

"What can we do that they can't do?"

"I hope to stop this plot once and for all," Thomas said.

"Why us? This doesn't sound like anything we belong around."

"Hear me out," Deer could sense the stress in Thomas' voice. "The general learned about it because the person he identified to us approached him to help. That person spent twenty years in the FBI, and until he disappeared, he had a contract position within the CIA. We think both individuals are now dead."

"But you think the plot continues?"

"That's right. Our initial theory was that the plotters would cover their tracks and forget about doing anything else. A sizeable task force within the Secret Service has worked on this twenty-four hours a day for the last couple of weeks. On top of that, I've had a small team looking at what the Service has uncovered in its investigation. This team has been making their own recommendations to me."

"I imagine the Secret Service isn't too happy about that."

"They didn't know it was happening, so there are no hurt feelings. I have no issues with the Service. It's just smart to have an extra set of minds analyzing the data. In this case, I'm very glad I did so. Last week, I became aware that data in the Secret Service investigative file is being tampered with. It's all kept in secure data storage, but you know as well as I that doesn't always mean much. Someone, maybe even an insider has done a pretty good job of changing a date here and there, deleting a name, an address, or something else."

"Can they recover the original data?" Deer asked.

"They don't fully realize the extent of the tampering, but their suspicions that something was going on is what flagged my shadow group to compare the original data they copied to what's currently in the Secret Service investigative file.   Over three hundred discrepancies, three hundred," he repeated and turned to face Deer, "were identified.   Some could be legit, but something definitely was going on. I needed time to attempt to trace who was making the changes."

"You didn't tell them about the compromise?"

"Four days ago, I sat right here with their Director and told him what I'm telling you. He loaned me one of his top computer forensic guys to be on the shadow team. That person is discreetly trying to prevent future unauthorized changes and is helping us trace the link that's been used to compromise the data. Within the Service, only a couple of people know of his involvement with us."

"If the hacker can change the data then he can read the data. He's one step ahead of the investigation."

Thomas nodded, "Or she."

"How does this come back to be something I should be interested in?"

"It's complicated. Every time the investigation starts to make progress the trail goes cold. Our best guess is that there are a few individuals up fairly high in Homeland Security and perhaps even the CIA and FBI who are involved in this."

"That's not good."

"No, it's not. I'd say the fanatics at both ends of the political spectrum are becoming more dangerous, except I see the spectrum as a circle, not a straight line. Whether you're a Stalin or a Hitler, you're still the exact same merciless dictator. Only your lies for doing what you're doing are different."

Deer had heard all this from Thomas before, and she had to agree with his logic, but she didn't like where this conversation seemed to be heading. She did not want to let her hunters loose on Americans.

Her small agency had been created to counter extreme threats against the United States, targeting individuals like foreign terrorists who posed an imminent threat. Even then her hunters would covertly seek out the target, but they would only be used if it appeared the targets would evade apprehension by a "more legitimate" law enforcement agency. If another agency could arrest or otherwise neutralize the target, the hunter would fade away without anyone ever knowing he or she was in the area. Deer used her hunters as a solution of last resort and reported their efforts to no one.

"You don't need to hear all the details, but suffice to say we've got an educated guess on a small number of those who might be involved. No proof and no hard evidence we can use against them, but we can neuter them in the old fashion way." A small smile formed on Thomas' face. "Four senior government employees are receiving promotions right now that will give them new positions in different agencies without access to anything relating to a national security issue. You'd be surprised how many government agencies exist. Finding spots to isolate them was quite easy."

"You think moving these four will stop everything?" Deer asked.

"Not exactly. Others are being shuffled around within their own agencies, but with less drastic impact on their careers. It's a wide net, but it's one that should work and have the least impact on the innocent. I think whoever is involved will take the hint and not start any new plotting against the president."

Deer waited throughout the pause in conversation. She didn't feel like repeating her question about his need for her help.

"You knew a guy named Reed Whatley from your early days, right?" he asked.

The name took her back almost thirty years. "Yeah, a loose cannon. Almost got me killed in Berlin. I thought he was fired."

"He was, but for the last ten or so years, he's used his international contacts to feed information, mostly low-level intelligence, to us in exchange for a tidy little profit. He's maintained his US citizenship but has bounced around Southeast Asia for most of the last two decades. For whatever reason, the Agency kept dealing with him even though our own files question his integrity and his loyalty."

"So, he's involved?"

"Long story, but we believe he is. We think he's working with the North Koreans in an effort to assassinate the president during his state visit next week to South Korea."

"Has the Secret Service recommended the trip be cancelled?"

"It's been suggested, but our theory has too many holes."

"Can't they simply pick up Whatley up for questioning?" Deer asked.

"He's out of the country and bouncing around in Asia. Timing is too limited, and there is no room for error."

The two discussed the situation for another ten minutes before Deer left to return to her office in the basement of the US Marshall Service building. Thomas stayed for a good half hour watching the river flow by before he went directly home.

Deer didn't mention the conversation to anyone on her small staff. Instead she closed her door and placed a flash drive into her computer. Thomas had told her that if she inserted the flash drive into any USB port besides the ones on her office computer, the flash drive would immediately reformat itself and all the information on the flash drive would be destroyed. He specified which computer in her office she needed to use to open the file. That impressed her since to her knowledge he had never been to her office.

He told her that any attempt to copy the file or print its contents would also result in an instant reformatting of the flash drive. Deer didn't think these precautions had anything to do with the trust that Thomas had in her. In fact, she liked this new level of security, only slightly less secure than her own.

No paper or digital trail existed on any of her hunters' activities. No formal approval process existed. The activities of her office were not briefed to anyone, not even Thomas. Her hunters were all identified on government employment and pay records as intelligence analysts for the U.S. Marshall Service.

The office did publish the routine intelligence information reports to support its cover role, but the information in these reports was not collected by any agents in the field. Rather, Deer's office picked out small pieces from the information contained in a large variety of recently published intelligence by other U.S. and allied agencies that pertained to a specific threat and combined that information into a single, focused report.

While Deer had received the very rare tasking from Thomas, the vast majority of her team's work had been at her direction. For the first few years after 9/11, the National Security Advisor had received a few briefings and had even initiated one of her agency's operations. These top national leaders quickly realized that while Deer's hunters could be very effective, it made political sense to know less and less about what they did. The most recent election placed a couple of administration turnovers between the decision to implement Deer's agency and today's environment.

Deer believed the last and this current administration would close her shop down in a blink of an eye, if they learned what it was really doing. She thought Thomas felt the same way, and had kept the specifics of her agency hidden among the few hundred deeply classified governmental endeavors that his boss and the president would be briefed on if a need presented itself.

Fortunately, those at the very top had little free time to be briefed on what was politically hot at the moment, and these "lesser" activities never made it onto the agenda. Deer knew a few other agency chiefs and special project managers who fought hard to get thirty seconds to brief their achievements to the president and had simply been told there was no time. They were welcome to write a short brief for the leadership to read when they had the time, but that was it.

Deer smiled at remembering something she had been told that the former president had said after learning that a terrorist bent on setting off a bomb at an American airport was killed in Canada.

"Great news," the president had said. "If we had anything to do with his death, I don't want to know about it."

Deer imagined Leon Thomas had that quote recorded somewhere in his files.

She returned her focus onto the computer screen. The information displayed from the flash drive intrigued her. Set forth in a series of very short paragraphs without any substantiating background, the information appeared to be a series of conclusions that led the author to believe that Reed Whatley would be meeting with a team of North Korean agents. The meeting would take place in South Korea in a few days, during which Whatley would provide the agents information on the president's itinerary along with a recommendation for the best two or three places to carry out the assassination.

The author claimed Whatley had already been paid a substantial amount of money, and a large sum of money had been transferred to a bank account in Hong Kong that the North Korean Intelligence agencies used. No specifics were provided.

The four main suspects masterminding the attack had already started taking steps to distance themselves from each other and the plot. They had even gone as far as losing or destroying each of their cell phones. Their new phones did not list each other as contacts, and all email traffic between the individuals had been deleted. The four had purchased new laptops or tablets.

The author of the document believed this indicated the planning phase had ended and the assassination plot had moved into operational mode. Deer agreed.

Deer reread the document and jotted down a few notes. Despite the fact that Deer hadn't conducted a field operation on her own in five years, she knew that she needed to personally carry out this assignment. She knew Whatley and was convinced she would recognize him. She had also never targeted one of her hunters at a US citizen before and didn't want to start now.

She opened her door. "Buzz, Dolly, I need to see you both."

The two joined her in her office. They had been with her almost since the beginning. While a couple others had also worked as part of the staff, they had retired and only came in occasionally as part time support when needed. Although all members of the staff were crucial to the team, none of them had ever been hunters.

She noticed that Buzz looked tired. "You okay, Buzz? You look like you're hung over."

Buzz smiled. "Allergies or something, haven't slept good the last two nights."

"Well, you can stay home tomorrow, but then I need you here the rest of the week."

"I don't need tomorrow off. I'll be fine."

"Okay, your call. Dolly, I need you to get me on a flight to Seoul tonight using one of the aliases that we've set up."

"When do you want to come back?" Dolly asked.

"I'm not sure. How about we set the return flight for Sunday and put me on a flight to Manila. I'll overnight there and then catch a flight back here."

"Do you want to go to Korea via Manila?" Dolly asked.

"No, no time," Deer said.

"You sure you want to do this?" Buzz asked.

She knew he realized that she was assigning a mission to herself.

"Yes. It's better this way. I'll stay in touch. The few things I need will be brought in under the radar by the Air Force. I'll pick them up at Osan Air Base."

"Dolly, one more thing, do you know if there's a good place to get my hair done around here?"

"Do I? But, you don't wear your hair the way I do. No offense, I like your hair, but it's been the same since I met you."

"So, let's change it," Deer said, smiling at Dolly's remark.

CHAPTER 3

The sound of a truck horn in the street below caused Deer to jump. She needed to quit looking back over the past few days and get moving. Her head throbbed, but she forced herself to get dressed and start packing. When she finished, she took a couple Tylenol tablets and sat down again. Like a force of its own, her mind went back to the day before.

She knew she had screwed the mission up. Everything went according to plan until she caught up with Whatley. She knew this final part would be difficult, but she had made it more difficult on herself than necessary. Twice in the afternoon she had followed him to spots where he was alone and she could've terminated him, but despite her own dislike for the guy, she wanted some proof that he was meeting with the North Koreans.

It took her missing those two opportunities to realize how illogical it was to wait for proof. The transfer of information didn't need to be made in person. It could be done by dead drop or through a third person. She didn't believe he would transmit anything over wire or the airwaves that could be intercepted or later traced. It would be done in person, but it didn't have to be done face to face with a North Korean. Furthermore, Deer knew she couldn't tell a North Korean from a South Korean.

Late in the afternoon, Whatley's movements became suspicious. He started looking around more and took some basic counter surveillance measures. She would have to make her move soon.

The small, state of the art camera that had been built into a sunglass strap and positioned on the back of her neck allowed Deer to maintain a distance from Whatley whenever he was somewhat stationary. As the camera linked to her phone, she could fiddle with her phone as though she was thoroughly absorbed with it and never look around for Whatley. She could stand or sit somewhere and not have to face him. The camera allowed her to zoom in and see him better than she could with her own eyes. It also had night vision capability, albeit somewhat limited.

As darkness descended on Pyongtek, Whatley suddenly waved down a taxi and drove off. Deer had anticipated the need for mobility and had been following Whatley around the city with the use of an old, beat up motorbike. It looked in bad shape which helped in making it of little interest to the casual observer, but the engine and a few other key components were in good running order. While it took her a few seconds to get to the bike, she easily weaved through traffic and caught up with the taxi. Traffic in Korea, even in these medium size cities, never moves very fast.

The taxi drove out of Pyongtek and headed northeast. Deer had no problem staying hidden in traffic until they left the outskirts of the city and traffic thinned. She kept well back and lost sight of the taxi on a few occasions. The taxi's brake lights lit up ahead of her when the taxi approached a roadside restaurant. Deer pulled off the road and turned off the engine of the bike killing its light as the taxi pulled into the parking lot.

The restaurant's parking lot had sufficient lighting to allow Deer to watch Whatley as the taxi drove off. She expected him to enter the restaurant, but he walked around the building and down what looked like a trail behind it. She parked the bike near the restaurant and followed him.

The lights from the building illuminated the first thirty or forty yards of the trail, so Deer stayed off to the side of the trail in the trees until she felt it was dark enough to move onto the trail. Despite the initial distance between them, she had little trouble spotting him. Whatley used a flashlight to see his way which made following him easy. He walked at least a quarter mile before he came to a clearing that had been set up as a picnic area.

Deer slowed her pace when she neared him and observed four large wooden picnic tables with attached benches in the clearing. Whatley sat on the table closest to her. He had placed the flashlight, which was still on, next to him on the table facing away from the trail and was doing something with his phone.

Deer walked toward him and fired two rounds from five yards into the side of his head. With his eyes fixated on the glare of the phone's screen, she didn't think Whatley ever noticed her coming. Despite the sound suppressor on the CZ82, she worried about someone hearing the gunfire. She checked the body for anything written or any portable storage device that Whatley may have intended to give to the North Koreans. She found a small paper tablet in a rear pocket of his pants that had annotations on the first sheet. The writing looked Korean to her, but she had no idea what it said. Other than his wallet and phone, he had nothing else on him.

She turned the flashlight off, stashed the notepad in her pocket, and picked up Whatley's cell phone. She had no intention of keeping it with her, but she wanted to get it away from the body and bury it.

"Whatley," a man's voice broke the silence around her.

It had come from the trail. A small flashlight beam suddenly broke through the darkness. Deer sprinted for the tree line opposite the trail. She heard a hushed conversation as she paused behind a tree.

She needed to circle around the two men she saw approach Whatley. Once around them, she thought she could get to the bike without drawing their attention. The darkness was both her ally and an impediment to her evading the men. She would be hard to see, but moving around them without making any noise would be difficult since seeing the best places to step would be nearly impossible in the darkness.

One of the men said something in Hangul, the local language, but she didn't understand him. The two directed their flashlights to the tree line and slowly scanned the area. Deer stayed low to the ground and backed further away from the men. She had to assume they were armed.

Suddenly, someone to her left turned on a flashlight and directed the small beam in her direction. Deer sprinted away and heard this new man say something.   Voices from her right responded, as well as from the direction of the two men near Whatley. She couldn't let them encircle her, or she would have to shoot her way out.

The further she ran away from the restaurant and her bike, the more convinced she became that Plan B was her only option to get back to her hotel.   Plan B meant forgetting about the motorcycle and walking or running back to her hotel.

After five minutes of running, Deer stopped and squatted near a small evergreen. She pulled a small container out of her pocket, rubbed her index finger into the black camouflage paint and rubbed stripes under her eyes and on her chin. Light rain began to fall.   Good, she thought, the rain would decrease visibility and would make it harder to hear her footsteps. She considered but discarded the idea of using the small camera that operated with her sunglasses and cell phone. The camera would give her some minimal night vision capability but only with a very narrow focus. The sunglasses would make everything else around her even darker, if that was possible, and use of the cell phone would only illuminate her to her pursuers.

Holding her phone close to her she turned it on to verify her position and the direction back to Pyongtek. It would be a long hike, but she didn't think the men had followed her this far away from the restaurant. Thirty steps later she learned how wrong she was as the beam of a flashlight cut through the darkness. Deer instinctively ducked and rolled behind a tree trunk too narrow to be much good. A round smashed into the tree and wood fragments sprayed in the air in front of her face.

The fool still had his flashlight on, and Deer placed two rounds into his chest. She started running away from the man before his limp body hit the ground.

Loud voices in the hotel's hallway brought Deer out of her semi-sleep and stopped her reliving the events of the night before. She went to the bathroom and splashed some cold water on her face. She had to leave.

CHAPTER 4

"A great way to end a mission," Deer said aloud in the empty room. She stood up and the dizziness returned. "Dammit," she took a sip of water before reaching for her phone. She sent a text to Buzz and double checked the room.

Despite the late hour in Washington D.C., Buzz still sat at his desk in the office when his phone buzzed. He glanced at the short text and called Dolly.

"You out on a date?" he asked her when she answered the phone.

"No, he had to do something with the wife and kids. What's up?"

Buzz felt pretty sure she was only kidding him when she made her comments about dating married men, and he didn't want to know anyway, but it still bothered him a little. He thought she knew it bothered him, and that was why she liked to tease him. He didn't consider himself a prude, and the two of them had never been more than coworkers, but still it got under his skin.

"If you don't mind, I need you here in the office."

"I'll be there in a few minutes," she said without questioning him and hung up. They had worked together for fifteen years, and while Buzz might be hesitant to call them more than coworkers, Dolly considered Buzz her friend. She also knew that if he called her at home and asked her to come into the office, he had a very good reason.

Dolly lived a short ride on the DC Metro away the office, and true to her word, she entered the office twelve minutes after the call.

"We have a problem. Deer needs help getting out of South

Korea and has requested one of the hunter's assistance."

"That doesn't sound right. What was she doing there?" Dolly asked. Despite asking the question, she turned her computer on and got ready to work.

"I'm not sure," Buzz said. He knew she had arranged to make the trip to Korea immediately after meeting with Thomas. Whatever this was, it was extremely sensitive and very important. "She felt that it was something she had to do personally and immediately."

"So, she didn't even tell you why she was going there?"

"No, but between you and me, that's why I asked you to send Clint to Hawaii. Deer hasn't taken on an operation in several years. Long ago she told me that she needed to stay here, that she couldn't afford to be in the field in case a crisis occurred that required her presence here."

"Has anything happened in Korea?" Dolly asked.

"I've been all over the net and the intel feeds, and I can't see a thing."

"What do you want me to do?"

"Get Clint to Busan, South Korea, as fast as you can. He'll meet Deer there. Then we need to get them both to Guam ASAP. She needs medical attention."

"Cripes."

"Let me read you her text," Buzz said and looked at his phone. "Hey, lousy head cold has me down. May need some help traveling home and would like to leave in a day or two. Would rather see a specialist than just a local doctor here in Busan."

"I don't like the sound of that."

"The text came from the city of Pyongtek, nowhere near Busan. She spent last night outdoors. Her track looks like she may have been running from something," Buzz offered his phone to Dolly.

She waved the offer off. "Sounds like she may be hurt."

Buzz nodded. "That's what I think."

One of the three computer screens on Buzz' desk chimed. His eyes went immediately to the screen. "Four men were found dead just outside Pyongtek early this morning. One appears to be a westerner and the other three Korean. All had been shot. No, three had been shot and one stabbed to death. Local police have no leads, but due to the number of victims, the Korean National Police have taken an interest."

"Any names yet?" Dolly asked.

"No, but I bet my lunch this is what I've been looking for."

"Can't believe she went up alone against four targets. What kind of weapons package did she take?"

"I have no idea. She said she would have some stuff she could pick up at Osan, but I did some snooping and couldn't find where she had set anything up."

"That makes no sense," Dolly said.

"She met with Leon Thomas the day she left. He must have directed the operation and managed the support package."

"Has that happened before?"

"In the early days, but not for years. Nothing about this has been normal. Unfortunately, we can't simply pick up the phone and call Thomas," Buzz said.

"Deer's alive and on the move. You haven't seen anything about the Korean security services locking down the country, have you?"

"No, but they are already on heightened security status due to our president's visit," Buzz stopped talking and looked at Dolly. "This has to be connected. How soon can we get Clint to Busan?"

Dolly turned to her computer and got to work.

"If he hurries, we can get him on a flight that's leaving in three hours."

"Do it," Buzz said. He grabbed his phone to call Clint Smith.

"Want me to set up a logistics package?" Dolly asked.

Buzz knew she was talking about weapons and other

specialized technical equipment. Normally, she wouldn't even ask, but they both knew this wasn't a normal operation.

"No, we better not. I think she just needs someone to physically help her move from spot to spot."

"She's going to get to Busan by herself," Dolly said. "Is there a chance we're missing something in the text?"

"Of course, but I think we've got it right. If she's involved with the four dead guys, she knows she needs to get away from the Pyongtek area as soon as she can. She can't wait for help. If I were her, I'd be on the first train out of there."

"She will be," Dolly said.

"I'll keep the track on her phone live. Once she's on the move, we'll know. "

"Let's hope that happens soon."

"Fortunately, male chauvinism in Korea is still alive and well. The last thing they'll be looking for is a lone woman shooter."

Dolly smiled at Buzz' remark. "You go, girl," she said half to herself.

"I think once she gets to Busan, she's home free. It's a big city, over a couple million people with plenty of spots to keep a low profile for a day or two."

"You know, we had her going through the Philippines, but we could send her to Japan as well as Guam for medical help," Dolly said.

"Let's do Guam. We've got a contact there, a doctor, who can help us keep this discreet. See if you can get them both on something leaving in two days."

Dolly started searching for flights, and Buzz walked across the room before punching the button on his phone that dialed Clint. Buzz looked around at the office and thought for the hundredth time how nice it would be if they could be a larger agency with a charter that allowed them overt support from the rest of the government. At the same time, he knew how impractical that would be. They wouldn't have lasted this long.

No one could hide or even sugarcoat the fact that the hunters, while used only as a last resort, were assassins. Even if they survived a change of administrations, someone with an uncompromising moral compass or with a political axe to grind would mention Section's existence to Congress, or worse yet, the press.

CHAPTER 5

Deer looked around the hotel room before leaving. She saw nothing that would leave a trail to her or anything that could link her to the deaths of the men from the night before. The blood stain on the carpet now hidden under the bed couldn't be seen, and she guessed it would be months, if not longer before someone moved the bed. By then, the stain would fade and dry and draw little interest.

For once she was glad she wasn't a tall, vivacious super model. She believed she was average in size and appearance and felt she wouldn't draw anything but a casual glance from most. Deer steeled her body to ignore the pain and move about as though nothing was wrong with her, and she hoped the makeup she used to cover the bruising to her face worked.

She took a taxi to the train station and purchased a ticket for the first train leaving the city. Bound for Taegu, a large city in the center of the country, Deer knew she would have no trouble there getting a connection to Busan. The train had enough empty seats to allow Deer to find a semi private spot in the back of one of the cars. For the first time in twenty-four hours, she felt like she could relax. Closing her eyes, she fell asleep before the last buildings of Pyongtek were behind her.

If she had known a man followed her onto the train and now watched her from a few rows away, she might not have fallen asleep so quickly.

In her defense, Deer knew very little about the assassination plot, but then how was she supposed to know that when the North Koreans agreed to assassinating the President of the United States, the young dictator in the north had thought it a terrific idea? He believed it could be one of his nation's greatest achievements. Not only would he be striking a decisive blow against the world's greatest superpower, he would be shaming his brothers to the south who would have failed to protect their most distinguished guest.

In fact, the killing of the U.S. president had become a top national priority. He directed the infiltration of a dozen of his best operators into South Korea and activated a number of his country's sleeper agents who lived in the south. He selected Yi Sung Minh to lead the mission and personally made it clear how it important it was to succeed.

Yi knew failure was not an option. The mission would end in either success or death. Possibly both, but there would be no backing away from the attempt, and he knew from the start that the mission had little chance for success. The Americans were quite good at keeping their president safe, and the South Korean government would throw hundreds of security forces into an outer perimeter making getting to the president nearly impossible. The American Whatley had promised to identify a weak spot in the president's itinerary along with a suggested way to exploit it.

When Yi found Whatley dead on top of the picnic table with nothing on him that would help with the mission, he felt his gut twist into a knot. The North Koreans didn't even have the American president's itinerary. How could they plan an attack when they didn't know when and where the man would be?

One of his team spotted a lone person fleeing from the scene, giving Yi a sliver of hope. Whatley had promised to provide information critical to the attack. It only made sense that the information was documented in some format that Whatley could hand to Yi.

It didn't matter to Yi if the information was on a CD, a flash drive, or simply written on a piece of paper. He needed that information. Whatley didn't have it, so it seemed logical to Yi that the person fleeing from the scene must have taken it. His team of five agents started their pursuit, and Yi felt optimistic that within the hour they would have their prey in hand. Yet, the night had ended in disaster. Whatley's assassin had killed three of his five agents. Well, Yi found one of the three alive but close to death, and while Yi had little doubt his agent would die within the hour, he shot the man in the head in anger after the man told Yi they were chasing a woman. Infuriated that a woman could be ruining their mission and evading his team, Yi spent another frustrating hour pursuing her, before he realized that he needed to come up with a better plan than running around at night in the rain.

Before he died, his agent had told him that he thought he had hit her with one of the rounds he had fired at her. Yi decided to send all seven of the agents he held back in reserve from the planned meeting with Whatley into Pyongtek to look for her. He would also have the two sleeper agents in the area help them. They would keep their eyes on medical clinics and pharmacies, as well as the bus and trains stations. A lone, injured American woman couldn't be that hard to find. His agent had even given them a basic description: Caucasian, average height and build.

Yi tasked one of the two North Korean sleeper agents, Pak Sung Anh, to watch the train station. Pak considered the assignment a waste of time. Unlike Yi who had never been to Pyongtek before, Pak knew thousands of Americans worked at the large US military installation situated on the outskirts of the city. He knew he would see dozens of American women at the train station throughout the day. The description wouldn't help him.

However, shortly after noon, a woman walked right by him and grabbed his attention. She had bruising on the side of her face that her makeup only partially concealed. He wasn't told to watch for that, but its presence drew his attention. Pak studied her, and after a few minutes, he came to the conclusion that she had something else wrong with her. He couldn't see a specific injury because the woman wore clothing that covered her arms and legs, but the way she walked and moved her arms made him suspicious.

Pak called Yi when the woman climbed aboard a train destined for Taegu. Yi instructed him to follow her and keep her in sight. He said he would be there in a few minutes, but the train left before Yi arrived.

At the station, Yi had to make a quick decision. If he sent some of his agents after the train, he would weaken his search capability in Pyongtek. He had decided to send two of his men by car to Taegu and keep the rest for the search, when a call from a source within the Korean National Police changed his plans. His source told him that the bodies of his dead team members had been discovered, and the KNP was sending a task force of twenty police officers to help the local police. Yi had hoped that the bodies wouldn't be discovered for a day or two. He knew that once the dead team members were found, it wouldn't be long before suspicions grew that the men had come from the north. Under clothing, dental work, and other things would give them away.

Remaining in Pyongtek would put them all at risk, so Yi decided to put all his chances on the woman one of the sleeper agents was now following to Taegu. A good break, he thought, but it would have been better if he had one of his assassins on the train with her. The sleeper had neither the skill nor the training to eliminate the woman and find out what she carried with her. He contacted his team members ordering all but two of them to drive to Kimhae, a small city, thirty miles north of Busan. He instructed the other two to meet up with him. They would try to reach Taegu before the train arrived. If they didn't, he hoped his man following her had enough skill to not lose her in Taegu.

CHAPTER 6

Deer opened her eyes when the train braked and shuddered as it passed by a train heading in the opposite direction. Her head throbbed and her arm felt numb. She could see a large city ahead as the train rounded a bend and continued to decelerate.

She scanned the passengers in the train and noticed an older man a few aisles away looking at her. He turned away as soon as she spotted him. Deer tensed. She knew it could mean nothing, but she also knew that she had to make sure he didn't follow her once they got off the train. He didn't look like a police officer or anything similar, but she had learned decades earlier not to let appearances fool her. Her first and last lesson in assuming someone's appearance could be trusted almost resulted in her death.

Deer could grin now about that learning experience, but back then it was no laughing matter. She had followed two men the CIA believed were involved in weapons smuggling as they walked through downtown Athens. Part of a three-person CIA team taking turns in their positions behind the two men, Deer had rotated to the position closest to the men when they disappeared down an alley.

She reached the alley barely twenty seconds after the two men had entered it; however, she saw nothing but a young teenager holding what seemed to be a baby wrapped in a blanket. The teenager leaned against the wall of a building a few steps from the street and appeared to be begging. Deer paid little attention to her, and for her mistake, she received a blow to the back of the head that sent her sprawling onto the pavement and into unconsciousness. The last thing that registered in her mind was what looked like a rolling pin, similar to what her mom used to flatten baking dough, swinging in the young woman's hand.

The blow to her head kept her off duty for the rest of the week, and the two men they had been following disappeared for nearly a year before being seen in Prague where the chase began anew. The young woman vanished and was never identified. Deer knew she was lucky to have survived the attack.

As the train approached the station, it slowed and most passengers got to their feet. In the commotion of people preparing to leave the train, Deer slipped out of her seat and went through the railcar's door to the next railcar behind her and away from the man. She continued walking through that railcar onto the next one before pausing to look back to see if the man had followed her. She saw him enter the railcar as she left it.

Passengers had already filled the next car's center aisle. She knew she could squeeze her way through the crowd, but a door to her right enticed her. She slipped into the empty bathroom and closed the door. She gave her pursuer what she thought to be enough time to walk past her before opening the door and peering out. The passengers had crowded into the space near the railcar's exit which made Deer's departure from the bathroom difficult, but she forced her way out.

She kept her head down and leaned forward a little hoping that the small crowd would help hide her. She didn't bother to look around. After another long minute the train came to a complete stop in the station. When the doors opened, the tide of passengers leaving the train carried her with them. Deer tried to stay within the thickest of the crowd while it moved toward the exits. She waited until she left the station to look for a place to decide what to do next.

Her decision depended on a number of things. She had planned to take the next train to Busan, but she needed to lose the person following her first. Her phone buzzed, and she looked at it.

"How's it going?" the text from Dolly read.

"Not sure," she replied and immediately regretted her choice of words. She did not want to get Dolly spun up. "Not feeling well and may have an unwelcome visitor later today unless I can find an excuse to avoid him. But for now, I'm fine."

A return text appeared almost instantly. "Wish I could be some help to u, but my husband is flying out of country to help a sick friend. I can't get away from the kids right now."

Deer grinned to herself. She knew right away whom Dolly referred to as her husband. Both she and Buzz had talked to Dolly about her infatuation with Clint Smith.

"If I see him I'll pass along your love."

"PLEASE DO!!!" Dolly replied.

Deer shook her head but still smiled. She entered a small restaurant that had a window facing the train station. She would give the man she thought was following her twenty minutes to realize he lost her trail before she would return to the station and get a ticket for the next train to Busan.

She ordered a coke and noodle soup while she waited. The man never appeared on the street, but she knew he could have left the station through a different door. When Deer finished the soup, she left the restaurant and returned to the train station. She didn't see any sign of the man. She purchased a first-class ticket on a train to Busan scheduled to depart in thirty minutes and went into the restroom to check on her bandages. If the man still searched for her, she knew he wouldn't look for her in the restroom. She remained in the restroom for twenty-five minutes before leaving.

The train to Busan arrived and departed on time. Deer ordered a large coffee once the train left Taegu. Exhausted, she wanted to sleep but knew she needed to keep her wits about her until she reached the safety of a hotel in Busan. She didn't expect Clint to arrive until the following morning, but she was certain once in a hotel in Busan she could relax. With any luck at all, she and Clint would be flying away from Korea in twenty-four hours.

While she didn't see anyone follow her onto the train, she had a nagging feeling someone was still out there watching her. For the first time, she wondered if she was being watched by the South Koreans. Had they found something to link her to the dead men? She couldn't think how they could've. Tracing her pursuit of Whatley, the night before, she didn't think anyone at the restaurant saw her, and she hadn't noticed any outdoor security cameras. She had left nothing behind, but then she thought of the motorcycle.

Just before arriving back at her hotel that morning, she had sent a message to the person who supplied the motorcycle to her telling him to retrieve it from the restaurant as soon as possible. She didn't know if the bodies from the night before had been discovered, but expected they had been by now. Whether or not her contact had retrieved the motorcycle before the police could've seized it, she didn't know, but he had told her it couldn't be traced. He didn't know her name. Still, she saw the motorcycle as her one weak link.

Two men entered the train car and took seats a few rows behind her. After an initial glance at them when she heard them enter, Deer kept her face looking forward. She put on her sunglasses and tried to position the small camera on the strap at them. The size of the first-class seats made it difficult, but from what she did manage to see, they didn't appear to have any interest in her.

She knew she needed to stay awake, but about an hour out of Busan, she fell asleep. The rocking of the train, her loss of blood and the low-grade fever she had developed overcame her best efforts to stay awake. The jerk of the train as it began to slow down in the city woke her with a start. Sweat balled up on her forehead and she felt nauseous. She looked around. No one looked back at her.

Her phone indicated she had missed an email. The only

emails that popped up on her phone originated from her office despite what internet address was displayed on the screen. This one had the return address of a travel agency.

"Sorry to inform you that the hotel reservations made for you have been cancelled for reasons beyond our control. We've replaced those reservations with one at the Hotel Dal. You should find this hotel more than satisfactory for your needs. Please let us know if we can be of additional service."

Deer smiled. She had left them with no knowledge of what she was doing or why. She guessed that they would know the name she used in Korea would not be the same name she traveled to Korea under, and that she had already made hotel reservations in Busan. They wanted to give her a choice, and she imagined the hotel they recommended would be a better fit for someone injured and on the run. She hadn't calculated that into her choice. In addition, if those following her were tracking her under the name she used in Pyongtek, it would be smart to mix things up a little. She decided to take the room at the hotel Buzz and Dolly recommended for her.

The train came to a halt and two men who concerned her left the train in a hurry. She cautioned herself not to get too relaxed. A mobile surveillance team would rotate who they had on her. She made a bee line for the taxis and grabbed one as it pulled up to the curb. She didn't bother to look around to see if anyone showed any signs of interest in her, but she did make note of the few vehicles that left the station at the same time and pulled up behind the taxi.

"Hotel Dal, please. Do you know it?"

"Yes. Are you okay?" the cab driver asked in very good English.

"Yes, I just have something bothering my stomach. Must be something I ate." Deer hadn't realized how obvious the symptoms from her wounds had become.

"That's easy to do here in Korea," the driver said grinning.

"Your English is excellent."

"My father was in the air force, the American one. My mom is from here, but I lived in America for most my life. I think my English is better than my Hangul," he laughed.

"Was he a pilot?" Deer asked.

"No, although he would've loved to have been one. He was enlisted. I'm in Busan working my way through veterinarian school."

"That's great. Will you practice here or go back to the States?"

"My plan is to return to Milwaukee."

"A beer drinker's paradise," Deer said, and the driver gave her a "thumbs up".

She grinned and glanced out the back window. She gave up any hope of determining if she had a tail. The two solid lines of slow moving cars behind her went on for blocks.

"What brings you to Korea?" he asked.

"Oh, just some personal stuff. A friend," she said and left it like that.

He glanced in the rear-view mirror, and Deer could see that he wanted her to elaborate. She didn't and hoped he would figure that the visit may not have gone as well as expected.

"I don't know if you know the city, but we're in the Nampo District of Busan which, by the way, I grew up saying Pusan with a P. Nampo is one of the larger districts, and your hotel is just outside it."

"Hopefully, not too far outside it."

"No, not like it's along the beach. There are a lot of nice hotels on the beach, but it gets really crowded there and takes longer to reach."

"Are the beaches nice?"

"Not the best in the world, but they're okay."

When he stopped in front of the hotel, Deer leaned forward and paid him an amount that included a sizeable tip. "Do you have a card or could you give me your number. I'll only be here for a couple days, but if I need a taxi, I'd rather hire a driver I know than take my chances."

"Of course," he said and handed her his card. "Please do call me."

Deer hurried into the hotel and never noticed the two men in a white Hyundai a half block away watching her.

CHAPTER 7

"You idiot," Yi snarled at the man standing in front of him in the Taegu train station. Construction on the highway from Pyongtek had delayed his arrival and already had him in a bad mood. "Why didn't you follow her onto the train?"

Pak Sung Anh bristled. Thirty or so years older than Yi, he expected a little more respect and appreciation for what he had done for Yi. Pak had spent the last forty years living in South Korea, and the absolute discipline mandated in the north had long been forgotten.

"She left the train station and then returned. You should be thankful I didn't lose track of her. I took pictures of her. I verified she was on the express to Busan, and then I waited for you as I thought you instructed me," Pak said with no fear in his voice.

Yi turned away and called the team members he sent to Kimhae. He instructed two of them to head to the Busan central train station and await further information and instructions.

"Show me the pictures," Yi said after he ended the call. He looked at them and felt more disgusted with his team. How did this ordinary looking woman do so much damage and then get away from him. He knew they needed the information that she may or may not even have on her anymore. The woman was insignificant; however, Yi wanted to personally punish her for putting him through this.

He also wanted to tear this old man apart with his bare hands. His insubordinate behavior infuriated him, but Yi knew he couldn't do anything here in the Taegu station, and he had no time to deal with him. After the mission, he would look Pak up and teach him some manners.

"Go home, and be thankful I don't have you killed right here."

Pak almost laughed at Yi. The station was swarming with people. He wanted to say something, but heeded the fragment of caution that had developed in his mind. He turned and walked away.

Yi walked over to his team members waiting by a kiosk and drinking coffee. "This is our target." He shared the photos of Deer that he now had on his phone. "I will be sending copies to all of you and the others. I've already sent them on to our men in Kimhae and instructed them to go to Busan. That's where the woman is headed. They should get to Busan ahead of her, and if they can't grab her at the station, they should be able to trail her."

Each of the three team members studied the woman's picture. A sneer formed on the lips of Kim Moon Jin.

"Once we get our hands on her, Kim, you can help me teach her that she should have never come to Korea," Yi said.

Kim nodded his expression turning into a grin. "We will get the opportunity, and I will make the most of it."

Yi thought most of the team sent with him to the south had the skills to carry out the mission, but only Kim seemed to have an absolute determination to succeed. He liked Kim and had known him for a few years, but he had never been with him on an operation. He had heard the legends that followed Kim, but this was the first time he had actually witnessed the focus and drive in the man. The night they pursued the woman through the darkness, only Kim pressed him to maintain the chase, even after Yi knew it was useless.

Yi thought Kim's scrutiny of the picture reminded him of the police dogs he had observed focusing on a scent in preparation for the hunt. Yi wished more on his team had Kim's drive and determination. He had little doubt that he could send Kim off on his own and the man would get the job done. The others needed to follow someone's direction.

Legend had it that a few years ago, Kim and three other North Korean agents were trying to sneak out of South Korea in the night after a mission when their boat engine died on them. After about an hour drifting at sea, a small South Korean patrol boat spotted them and approached cautiously. When the patrol boat pulled up next to the North Koreans, Kim slipped over the edge of the boat into the frigid water and swam around or under the South Korean boat. While the South Koreans focused on the three remaining North Koreans, Kim climbed on board the patrol boat killing two South Koreans with a knife before using one the dead men's weapon to kill the other three. The North Koreans drove the patrol boat to the north towing their own boat behind it.

Yi had always doubted the story. The water off the coast of was too cold to allow someone to last too long in the sea, and how did a person get up the side of even a small patrol boat? But why would all the agents say that he did it, and for that matter how could they have seized a South Korean patrol boat? They did return in one, and Yi had seen the boat on display a year later.

He might have felt a little threatened by Kim if Kim had any political ambitions at all, but the man had a reputation of not wanting anything but the job he had and sufficient compensation to let him live a comfortable life. While Kim had been a team leader for the last couple of years, his personnel file disclosed a history of not getting along with previous team chiefs he had worked under. Yi felt that might have been caused by the respective team chiefs being timid or indecisive. He had endured a few of those before he moved up in the ranks, so he could sympathize with Kim.

Yi's family had roles in the North Korean government for the past sixty years. This status gave Yi an advantage over most of his peers. On the other hand, Kim had come from a peasant background outside the capital. Many in the government had a natural bias against any commoner entering government service, and while Yi never had, he knew this background would limit Kim's rise in the intelligence service.

The express train the American woman was on had a thirty-minute start on Yi and his team, but as he had thought on the drive to Taegu, Yi now believed they might be able to beat the train to Busan. Traffic was light on the expressway and unlike the drive to Taegu, they reached the outskirts of Busan before the train. However, this city of over three million did not make it easy to get from the expressway to the train station. Late in the rush hour, getting anywhere fast on the busy streets was a near impossibility.

Yi had ordered his entire team to Busan, and he knew the two-man team he had positioned earlier in the town near Busan had already arrived at the station and now waited for the woman. They had orders to grab the woman as she left the station. If they couldn't, they were to follow and grab her at the first chance they had. Yi wanted her alive, but if necessary she should be killed and brought to him. His team had to have the information that she must be carrying with her. Yi didn't want to entertain the possibility this was the wrong woman or that she had already disposed of the information that Whatley had promised him.

While Yi's vehicle struggled through the traffic, ahead of him, his two men stood among the thirty or so other people waiting for the train's arrival at the Busan station. The passengers began leaving the train, and they saw the woman who matched the picture leave with them. Unfortunately, they waited for the train at a spot that had left them a good thirty yards from the door from which she emerged. The two moved as fast as they could to intercept her departure without raising attention to themselves. However, the throng of passengers leaving the train slowed their pursuit and forced the two to work their way through a surging crowd in its own hurry to get somewhere.

By the time the two men got outside of the station and away

from most of the crowd, all they could do was watch the woman climb into a taxi. Their bad luck reversed itself as the taxi drove slowly away in the direction toward where the men had parked their car two blocks away.

The men ran to their car and were rewarded by a stoplight that stopped the taxi, giving the two men enough time to reach their car without losing sight of the cab. They drove onto the busy road and followed the taxi, losing sight of the cab a couple times, but managing to find it each time. They gradually cut the distance to a four-car gap between them and the woman's taxi.

They saw the cab drive through a stoplight that changed red when the taxi passed under it. The cars in front of them stopped, and they watched as the taxi turned into a hotel's front entrance too far away for the two men to do anything.

"Damn this traffic!" Oh Chung Chin exclaimed.

"At least we know where she's staying," his companion said.

"I don't see how that woman evaded the team."

"She was lucky. Her luck is about to run out."

Oh nodded. Despite knowing the hotel in which the woman was staying, he dreaded making the call to Yi and telling him they had not been able to capture her. Oh wanted to get this mission over and to somehow survive. He understood his duty and would do it, but in the end, he wanted to still be breathing. He knew that Yi and especially Kim saw the entire team as pawns that could be sacrificed if it helped them reach their goal.

Oh had witnessed suicide bombers dispatched by ISIS leadership blow themselves up in Syria and knew of others deployed by the multitude of fanatical groups throughout that entire region. He had always thought how amazingly stupid these people were to allow themselves to become human bombs. In his mind, there was always a better way. Not that anyone in his chain of command expected Oh to strap on a bomb and blow himself up, but they would be willing to put him into some position that was tantamount to suicide to accomplish the mission.

"There is always a better way," Oh mumble out loud without meaning to.

"What?" his companion said.

"Nothing," Oh said. The man might agree with his point of view, but he might also mention his doubts about Oh's loyalty to Yi or Kim. After all, telling on one's peers was greatly appreciated and even rewarded throughout the government. What Oh thought to be common sense could be considered outright treason to someone else. He'd seen people shot or imprisoned for less.

"Should we follow her in?"

"She would be suspicious of us, and we might draw the attention of the hotel's security if we followed her in but did not get a room. She took her suitcase in with her, and the taxi has left. I think she is planning to stay. Let's see how Yi wants to handle this."

He called Yi and discovered that his leader had arrived at the train station. Yi instructed the two to find a spot where they could maintain a view of the hotel's entrance. If the woman left they were to follow. Yi would come to them and formulate a plan.

By the time Yi arrived at the hotel, he already had his plan. The list of sleeper agents he had been provided included a few in this large city, and two hours later, Yi and Kim sat in a small restaurant talking to a city police sergeant who had been a sleeper agent for North Korea for thirty years.

To say Sergeant Lee Lim Kwan was nervous would be an understatement. During the entire period of his association with the North, he had never done anything of substance for them. He had not seen a North Korean intelligence officer for twenty years.

"Calm down," Yi ordered for the second time. "We just need you to do something very simple for us." Yi's patience for these so-called North Korean supporters had reached his limit. He would definitely report to his supervisors how worthless they might prove to be in a real crisis.

Sergeant Lee's mind was churning and calming down was out of the question. He had done something very stupid when he was a college student. After a series of nationwide student riots and the subsequent police crackdown, he allowed himself to be recruited as a spy for the North Koreans. At that time, full of rage and "ideological purity," he believed he had done the right thing. It only took a few years for Lee to regret his decision. However, one couldn't quit being an agent for the North. He had provided a few pieces of innocuous information over the years to his North Korean handlers, and for the most part they had left him alone.

Until the recent phone call from Yi, he believed he would never be tasked to do anything significant for his North Korean handlers. He had somehow convinced himself in the last two decades that he wasn't really a traitor. How foolish that conclusion felt right now.

This latest alert from the North had not been that alarming, since he had received similar ones four times before. On each of those occasions, tensions between the two Koreas had almost brought them to war. Lee knew his handlers in the North wanted him to be prepared to sabotage the major utility systems in and around Busan. He had resented passing along the crumbs of information that he had, and he believed if war came, he would stand by his brothers in the South and die for the country he had come to love. He would never commit any sabotage for the crazy man up north. At least, that was what he told himself.

What this man Yi wanted didn't seem to pose any threat against Busan or his country, and what were his options? Sergeant Lee knew that telling this North Korean to get lost could ruin his life, and there were the threats.

"I need you to meet with the hotel management and identify this woman and learn her room number. That is all, but I need you to do it now," Yi said to him.

"It's not that easy," Lee replied.

"Yes, it is, and you have no choice," Yi hissed. "Remember

the consequences to your family, not only to you if you disobey now."

The man was under a lot of stress, Lee thought, but he knew the threat he made wasn't a bluff.

"I'll do it," Lee said.

"Make up any excuse you want, but it's urgent that I talk to this woman tonight."

"How do I get back with you to tell you the information you want?"

"Call me. You won't have to see me again."

Ten minutes later, Lee entered the Hotel Dal and sought out the night manager. His heart still raced, and he told himself to calm down or he'd have a heart attack. These men from the North only wanted this American woman. She must have done something that infuriated them, since they had chased her all the way to the southern tip of South Korea. He had theorized that the alert he had received from North Korea had something to do with the American president's visit. The timing and the gathering of agents in Busan fit with the visit.

He now wondered if this American woman might have something to do with the president's visit, or if his theory was wrong. Had the alert been entirely about this woman? Either way, this was between the North Koreans and the Americans. If he could convince himself of this, then maybe he could get rid of the guilty knot in his belly.

Fortunately, it turned out that the night manager had a nephew in the police force and readily complied with Lee's request. The manager barely glanced at Lee's credentials. Still the effort took some time. Finding the names of people who checked in within ten minutes of the time Yi had provided simply took a review of the registry data stored in the database. However, Yi had insisted that Lee identify the woman by any video footage the hotel might have. Retrieving and analyzing the front desk recordings to match the picture with the woman and with the room number took another half hour.

"She is in room number 834 and is registered as Sara Lynn, a US citizen. She booked the room for three nights," the night manager said.

"Thanks, please keep this inquiry to yourself. You know, police business," Lee said.

"Of course, I understand," the manager said.

Lee passed the information to Yi from the safety of his car. He hoped Yi would let him return to his home. The woman looked sick, and Lee now felt sick for helping Yi and his pack of wolves do whatever they had planned for this woman.

"We shouldn't need you again tonight, but stay by your phone," Yi said and terminated the call.

Sergeant Lee started his car and drove away from the hotel. Despite his years with the police force, he realized his hands had started shaking.

Yi wasted little time in sending in one of his men to get the layout of the lobby area, find the elevators, and take them to the floor where the American witch's room was located. His man did so and walked the hallway to locate the room before heading back to Yi and the rest of the team.

"What do you suggest, Kim?" Yi asked. He already had a plan in mind, but he wanted to get Kim's thoughts. The man had been on as many field operations as he had, perhaps more, and Yi wanted to reinforce Kim's role as his number two.

"Wait until late, say around midnight or a little after. Send in someone to rent a room and in doing so distract the night clerk. While the clerk is busy, three men walk in talking like they're coming in from a night on the city and go directly to the elevator. Proceed to the woman's room, get the information we need, kill her, and get out."

Yi wanted to say kill her slowly, but he knew Kim was right. The mission came first, and they were almost out of time. "Good. We'll do it just that way. We'll take the drugs in case we have to use them on her, we don't need her screaming her head off."

A few hours later, Oh Chung Chin entered the hotel lobby and proceeded to negotiate with the solitary late-night receptionist for the best price for a room.

"You know you won't get any more guests tonight, and I'll only be in the room for six hours," he said. He grinned at the clerk, a woman in her mid to late forties. "It might be worth a dinner out tomorrow."

"With you?' the woman laughed. She noticed but paid no attention to the three men who entered the hotel and went to the elevator. "For that, you may have to pay extra for the room."

Oh kept the woman talking until he realized he had to rent the room or become a real annoyance. As he walked to the elevator, he had to admit, he had gotten a good price for the room.

A few minutes past midnight, three North Koreans, led by Kim Moon Jin, approached the door to the room rented by Sara Lynn. Kim had a small tool in his hand that he had used with success in breaking into hotel rooms all over the globe. He looked at his two men and all three nodded. Kim popped the door open making almost no noise at all, and all three rushed in.

CHAPTER 8

Clint Smith climbed out of the hotel pool and grabbed the towel off his lounge chair to dry off. He picked up his phone and saw that he had missed a call and a text from Buzz. Sitting down on the lounge chair he returned the call.

"Hey, Clint, how's life in paradise?" Buzz asked.

"Just got here, I'll let you know in a week."

"Maybe some other time, we've booked you on a plane to Korea that leaves in a few hours."

"Are you serious?" Clint asked.

"Sorry, but I am. This is a special, and it's urgent."

"Sounds like it."

"There's no brief for this one. I've got nothing to bring you up to speed. We need you in Busan, Korea. There you'll meet up with Deer and help get her out of the country."

"Okay," Clint said. He had a lot of questions, but he held off for the moment from asking them.

"I don't have much more for you, Clint. At this point, there is no target, my best guess is that Deer took care of the targets and may have gotten injured in the process."

"She took on a mission by herself?"

"Totally. We know nothing about it here. Her message to us implied a need for help in getting to a doctor. That's about it. Once you reach her, you'll assist her in catching a plane out of there."

"Sounds simple enough," Clint said.

"I hope so, what? One-minute Clint," Buzz said. A few seconds later, he said, "Dolly told me to tell you she's got short black hair."

"Who, Dolly?"

"No, sorry about that, Deer cut her hair short and had it died black before she left here."

"Gotcha, anything else?"

"No, reservations are being transmitted to you right now. Any updates we get will be sent to you."

"You know, this means I'll miss the big luau tonight," Clint said.

"Get with the times, Clint. You can watch those online."

It only took Clint a half hour to check out and be on a taxi bound for the airport in Honolulu. A couple hours later, he watched from his window seat as the coastline of Honolulu disappeared behind him. He had never flown on Korean Air before and was looking forward to the experience. He was not looking forward to his mission.

A few minutes before takeoff, he called Buzz for an update. While he had been assured that no one anticipated any danger, Clint didn't like the idea of going into what had been an operational environment without any intelligence, without any weapon, and without a plan.

"She's injured in some way. Not so much that she couldn't get on a train, but it has to be bad enough that she needs help getting through airport security and out of the country. She needs to see a doctor," Buzz had told him.

"Are the South Korean authorities looking for her?" Clint asked.

"I've been looking for any sign of that and so far have not seen any. One of the dead was an American, so they've briefed the Embassy. No ID on the man yet. I'm seeing a little traffic that indicates some concern that the other three may be from North Korea. No ID on them yet either."

"Was the other American one of our hunters?"

"No."

"Why would she go up against four of them by herself, or do you think she was working with the other American?"

"Like I said, the American was not one of ours, and I'm not seeing any message traffic that would make me think he was working for any other allied service," Buzz said. "I don't think Deer knew she was going to encounter as many of them as she did. She traveled by vehicle to a spot near to where whatever happened happened. Her trace has her traveling down a road at a fairly good clip, but her return to her hotel was definitely by foot through the countryside."

Clint knew the phones they had enabled Section to trace their movements. "So you guys really don't know what she's been up to?"

"No." Buzz kept his theories to himself.

"Think she's been shot?" Clint asked.

"That's what I'm thinking. My guess is that she's got the wound covered and has stopped the bleeding, but doesn't want to be seen by a doctor in Korea. Could be a stab wound."

"We don't have a doctor we can use in Korea? One like Barbara," Clint asked, referring to a doctor who had helped him one time and who had since been an important person in his life.

"No. Our best option is to get her to Guam. We're working on tickets right now. Unless something unexpected happens, you'll spend less than twenty-four hours in Busan."

"Ok. So, I get a lot of frequent flyer miles. Guess it could be worse."

"Although you're traveling under your own name, she's under an alias. In country, she may even be using a different name."

"That's okay. When I see her, I'll call her Mom. That'll cheer her up," Clint said and Buzz laughed.

After the call, Clint let the mission escape his mind and focused his thoughts on Doctor Barbara White. She was the first woman in his life to make him think about settling down. He knew she cared for him, too, but their relationship started soon after she divorced a cheating husband. She didn't feel as though she could trust her feelings and had escaped the relationship with

Clint by volunteering to be part of a Doctors Without Borders mission in Africa. She would be returning to the U.S. at the end of the month, and Clint still wasn't sure if she wanted to continue their relationship or not.

At first, it had angered Clint that she had fled the country to get away from him. He had even written to her asking her why she left so abruptly. They hadn't made any commitment to each other. He finally realized, though, that the reason he had felt like he had about her unexpected departure was because he wanted that commitment. She may have sensed it, too.

"Are you in the military?" the man sitting next to him asked about an hour into the flight.

"I was, but I'm out now. How about you?" Clint figured the man had to be too old to still be on active duty, but he could be a civilian employee.

"Retired air force. I'm heading over to visit my daughter at Osan Air Base. She's a pilot in the air force."

Clint could sense the pride in his voice. "That's great."

"Too bad her mother can't see her today," the man said.

Clint kept his curiosity to himself.

"She passed away a few years ago," the man volunteered.

"Sorry," Clint said. He did feel bad for the man, but at the same time he wished the man would stop talking or at least change the topic.

"Does your daughter like to fly?" Clint asked, knowing it was a dumb question. He had met few pilots who didn't love flying.

"She's crazy about it." The man leaned his head back against the top of his seat and closed his eyes.

Clint liked window seats on planes because he enjoyed looking out the window. However, he usually grabbed an aisle seat due to his six feet two-inch frame. Buzz and Dolly knew his preference for aisle seats, so Clint guessed that the reservations were made late and there were none available. He didn't mind the inconvenience. He enjoyed flying, and like the man's daughter, he would've liked being a pilot.

Looking out the window, he didn't see a cloud in the sky and hoped it was a positive sign. He wondered what Deer had been up to and why she took on this mission without even discussing it with Buzz. He didn't come up with any decent theories until after the plane touched down in Busan, South Korea, where he encountered what he believed were heightened security measures.

"Is this normal or is something going on?" he asked a female flight attendant he recognized from his flight, who happened to be walking next to him.

"You're American?" she asked.

"Yes."

"Your president is arriving in two or three days. It will be the first visit ever of an American president to Busan."

"Oh, I guess I should've known that," Clint said, and suddenly the thought struck him that there had to be a connection between Deer's sudden trip to Korea and the president's visit.

"Will you be staying here long?" she asked. Her eyes seemed to smile as much as her lips.

"Only a couple of days. Meeting my mom here and then traveling around a bit. Is this your home?"

"Yes. It's a nice city. My parents have a restaurant I'd recommend," she took a card from a small purse she carried and handed it to Clint. "I have a couple days off. If I can do anything to make your stay more pleasurable, give me a call." She gave a slight wave before entering into a restricted area.

Clint glanced at the card and noticed on the back of the card she had written her name, May, along with a phone number. "Maybe next time," he said to himself and pocketed the card.

After retrieving his luggage, he looked for a semi-secluded spot to call Buzz. He thought he would have received some message by now telling him where to meet Deer, but he had received nothing.

CHAPTER 9

Clint laughed to himself after reading the text that arrived on his phone.

"Your date will meet you in room 834, Hotel Dal. Remember, it is your responsibility to ensure the privacy and cleanliness of the hotel and room before you accept our services. You already selected your date off our website. Once you enter the room, charges will be levied against your account, and there will be no refunds."

Clint guessed that Dolly sent the text. The texts and phones had the most sophisticated security software available built into them, but Section still had a habit of talking around the subject. Dolly, in particular, liked to get a little silly in some of her texts.

"Understand," he replied. He knew they only needed to give a room number and a hotel. The extra message told him to see if anyone had the hotel under surveillance. "Will you let her know I'm coming, or should I?"

"She already knows. She might be a bit apprehensive, but she won't turn you away."

Once Clint retrieved his luggage, he left the airport and joined the line of people waiting for taxis in the dark. Section hadn't made a reservation for him at the hotel. The more he thought about it, the more he felt it would be smart of him to check into a room first before approaching Deer. That would enable him to wonder through the hotel a little less suspiciously than someone walking off the street with no obvious reason for being there.

The cab ride only took fifteen minutes. Despite the late hour, a number of cars were on the roads and a few pedestrians still walked along the sidewalks. Another taxi pulled into the hotel entrance area as Clint paid his cab driver, grabbed his suitcase, and started to approach the hotel's front doors. An elderly American couple got out of the cab and began struggling with their luggage.

"Here, let me help you," Clint said and picked up the largest of the three suitcases.

"Oh, there's no need," the man said.

"Let him help, George," the woman said. "You've already been complaining about your back."

The man grunted something Clint couldn't understand. Clint took advantage of the time it took the woman to pay the cab driver and arrange her large purse to study the area around the front of the hotel. He saw a car parked on the other side of the road that had someone sitting in it, and a lone man leaned against the wall of a bank on his side of the street one block away.

The couple started walking to the hotel's entrance, and Clint followed them in. Once inside the man flagged down a young man wearing a uniform that indicated he was a hotel employee. The young man rushed over and began transferring the couple's luggage to a push cart.

"Thank you," the woman said as Clint left the two.

"No problem," Clint said.

The old man didn't say anything or even look in Clint's direction.

The hotel had rooms available, and Clint asked for and received a room as high up in the hotel as possible. The clerk gave him room 1002, telling him it was a special room and quoted him a price that he thought might make Buzz choke.

"Two nights," Clint said.

Clint went directly to his hotel room. He didn't notice anyone or anything suspicious inside the hotel. His room turned out to be a corner suite with the door to the suite opening to a room that a combined a living area with a small kitchenette. An interior door provided access to the bedroom with what appeared to be a king bed and an attached bathroom.

He threw his luggage onto the couch that looked like it could be pulled out and become a second bed. The room's windows gave him a good view of the city. The car in which he saw an individual hadn't moved from its spot across the street, but he couldn't tell if anyone was still in it. His angle of view prevented him from seeing if the person he observed earlier leaning against the front wall of the bank had moved or not. Scanning the area that he could see, Clint didn't notice anyone lingering suspiciously elsewhere outside the hotel.

He picked up the hotel phone and dialed Deer's room number.

"Hello." The woman's voice that came back through the phone sounded strained and weak. He couldn't be sure if the woman was Deer.

"Are you ok?" Clint asked hoping she would recognize his voice.

"Clint?"

"Yes, it's me. I'll be at your door in a minute. Will that be okay?"

"Yes," she said and hung up the phone.

CHAPTER 10

Other than Deer recognizing him on the phone, Clint didn't like much about the phone call. She sounded weak and tired, almost feeble. He went directly to her room and knocked. When she answered the door, Clint had to take a second to even recognize her.

"Come in," she said.

"Besides the bruise to your face, how are you hurt?" he asked while she sat down on the nearest chair.

"Shot in the arm. I think it may be getting infected. A few other lumps and scratches."

"I think we should get you to a doctor right now," Clint said.

"Not in Korea. Tomorrow we're flying to Guam. I'll last until then. I may need you to run out and get me a few things. You can buy a lot straight from a pharmacy here without going through a doctor."

"Are you sure?"

Deer nodded.

"Is anyone chasing you?"

"I think so. At least they were," she paused and for a second Clint thought she had stopped talking. "North Koreans. Between you and me and no one else, they've got a plot to assassinate the president. They were working with an American."

"An American?"

Ignoring the question, Deer continued. "The operation was a rush but too important not to do. I knew the American which made sense for me to take the mission. Don't look at me like that. I know I'm rusty, but this one came with no time to plan and had to be done. Besides, I won't send any of you after an American."

Clint let her words sink in. "I assume you accomplished your mission."

"Yes, but a team of North Korean agents showed up at the same time. Luckily, the target was paranoid enough to want to meet with the Koreans in person to hand deliver his information to them." She reached into her jacket pocket and pulled out a small, paper tablet.

"Not sure if this is even it. It's not in English, but we believe it provides information on how and when to best attack the president while he's here."

"We?"

"One other person. Let's leave it at that."

"I hope someone has informed the Secret Service."

"Yes, they know about an increased threat. They know nothing about this mission or us," Deer said.

"The president should just cancel his trip."

"You try to tell the president that. They're either afraid of everything or won't believe anything will ever happen to them. You know how they are."

Never having met a president in person, Clint didn't.

"Why the jacket in here?" he asked.

"My makeshift bandage is oozing. I don't want to leave anything around that might raise suspicions."

"I'll run out and get you a few supplies as soon as everything opens in the morning. By the way, there may have been a couple guys outside the hotel watching the entrance."

"Damn," Deer said. "They could be either the South Korean police or the North Koreans."

"So, we need to stay away from them either way."

"That's right."

"Are you armed," Clint asked.

"Not anymore, had to ditch everything I had after the mission."

Clint nodded but didn't like their situation.

"Hey, at this point we wouldn't know if we were shooting at

allies or enemies," Deer said.

"Can't we just walk into the consulate and ask for help getting home?"

"Too big of a risk. Timing would be terrible, and my wound would link me, us, to the deaths in Pyongtek. It wouldn't prove anything, but it would make anyone with only a little sense awfully suspicious, and we don't need that. I'd rather lose my arm."

Clint believed her. "Okay, but let's get you out of here. It would be too simple to trace you to this room if someone did follow you. No way they can link me to you. Let's head to my room right now."

Deer nodded. "Let me get my stuff."

"I'll come back and get it. The faster I get you out of here and cleaned up, the better I'll feel."

"Okay," she said, but she still grabbed her backpack before following Clint out of the room.

"How much do Buzz and Dolly know about all this?" Clint asked once they were in the elevator.

"Only that I'm here and need help getting out. They may have guessed a lot of the rest by now."

"Have you passed the information in the note on to anyone?"

"Not yet. We have time, but we should get it to them soon. It's more important to not allow the North Koreans to get it. Hell, I'm only assuming what I found on Whatley is more than a recipe for fried rice. Read Hangul?"

"No," Clint said and opened the door to his hotel suite.

"Damn, I need to talk to Dolly. She's fixing you up with better rooms than I get."

Deer sat down on the nearest chair, and Clint noticed that she looked paler than she did in her room.

"Let's take a look at this wound of yours."

She nodded but did little to help him as he took the jacket off her. The blood had oozed through the makeshift bandage and stained the sleeve of her blouse. The sleeve clung to the bandage. Without asking, Clint took the small pocket knife out of his pocket and cut the sleeve from the rest of the shirt.

"Don't let the blood get on the chair," Deer said. Her voice sounded strained and came out almost as a whisper.

Clint placed her jacket over the arm of the chair. The wound had stopped bleeding so he wasn't too concerned about getting blood on the chair, but he understood her concern. He unraveled the bandage, having to cut part of it apart, and studied the wound. It looked nasty. The round had gone through the arm. Clint had enough experiences with wounds in the military to know this one needed immediate attention.

"Can you make it into the bathroom? I need to try to clean this."

"I'm not dead yet." She stood and followed Clint into the bathroom where she sat down on the toilet.

Clint soaked a wash cloth in the sink and started to blot the wound. Water and blood streamed down onto the tile floor.

"Wait a second," Deer said. "Bring me the backpack and give me a second alone."

Clint did and while Deer was alone in the bathroom, he sent a short text to Buzz. "Patient is with me but does not look well. Getting to doctor by tomorrow is imperative."

"You can come back in," Deer called from the bathroom.

She had changed into what she might wear to a gym to work out, shorts and a sports bra. She stood in the bathtub, leaning against the wall. "Now you can spill all the blood you want."

Clint looked at the floor around the toilet and saw that Deer had already cleaned the area up. He also noticed something else he didn't expect, a nasty gash across her gut.

"How's your stomach?"

"Just a graze. I'll wash it after you finish with my arm."

"You should see yourself. Between the black eye and swelling and the two wounds you look like –"

"I've seen myself. You ought to see the other guy," she forced a grin.

"There's a mini bar in the room. You may want a drink first. I need to clean the area around the wound, and I imagine it'll be tender."

"I hope you're talking about my arm."

That caught Clint off guard, and he smiled. "Yes, ma'am, your arm."

"Grab a variety," she said.

Clint left and returned with a handful of tiny bottles. Deer scrubbed the belly wound with a soapy wash cloth before she took the shower head that was attached to a flexible hose and sprayed water to rinse off the soap.

"Got any vodka?" she asked

Clint opened a bottle and offered it to her along with a glass. She took the tiny bottle but not the glass before lying down in the tub. Clint watched as Deer drizzled vodka over the now bright red scar that ran several inches across her. She grimaced and inhaled with a hissing sound as the vodka made contact.

"Not exactly doctor recommended," Clint said.

"Don't you ever watch any old westerns? If it's good enough for John Wayne, it's good enough for me." She struggled back up to a standing position and extended her wounded arm.

Clint saw small sweat droplets form on her brow and the color start to go out of her face. He placed his hands under her armpits.

"This will be easier if you sit down," he said and started to kneel down.

Deer needed no further encouragement and sat down in the tub.

"Are you going to be okay?"

Rather than say anything, Deer nodded. Clint opened and offered her another small bottle. Deer drank it in one big gulp.

"Ugh! I hate gin." She shook her head, but her face got some of its coloring back. "Ok, do what you've got to do."

Clint thought back to all the first aid training he had received and a few life experiences. He tried to be gentle, and he knew Deer was one tough woman, but the flushing of the wound and rubbing the skin surrounding it brought more than a few gasps and groans. When he finished Deer leaned back against the side the tub. Clint thought she might have passed out.

"I'll be right back," he said.

Deer didn't answer.

Clint took a clean black tee shirt out his suitcase and used his knife to cut it down to form a length of material long enough to wrap multiple times around Deer's arm. He folded it into three layers. He considered folding it into four layers, but decided to go for width around the wound rather than another layer of depth. He looked in Deer's backpack and found the black electrical tape she used on the makeshift bandage she had made.

He returned to the bathroom with the new bandage and the rest of his tee shirt. Deer hadn't moved but her eyes were open, and she appeared more alert.

"How are you feeling?"

"Lousy, but I'll survive another day."

Clint wanted to say you might, but your arm might not. Instead, he said, "I need to blot the wound a little before I wrap it."

Deer sat up and extended her arm. She watched Clint blot the area immediately around the wound removing the fresh streaks of blood. He wrapped the wound and fastened it with the tape.

"Too tight?"

"No."

"That should keep your arm from falling off for a day or two," Clint said.

"Not a good joke."

Clint felt like saying what joke but instead helped her out of the tub and gave her a new towel to dry off.

"What pain killers do you have?" he asked.

"In the backpack."

Returning to her pack he found a bottle of extra strength Tylenol. Hardly sufficient, he thought, but returned to the bathroom with the Tylenol. She took three pills with a glass of water.

As if reading his mind, she said, "In the morning, I'll need you to get some type of antibiotic and a better pain killer for me."

He walked her out of the bathroom to his bed.

"I can sleep on the couch," she said but offered little resistance as Clint gave her a gentle push.

He covered her. "I guess we should keep your sleeping in my bed a secret," Clint said smiling.

"Oh God, yes, it would break Dolly's heart."

It took Clint a few seconds to understand what Deer meant. He barely knew Dolly, and other than the one day in Paris, France, had never been around her. He imagined it was an inside joke he wasn't privy to. It didn't matter. He left Deer in the bedroom and closed the door to the room behind him. In the outer room of the suite, he sat down and sent a text to Buzz.

"Have her with me in my room. Safer here and I was able to tend to her wounds. Seeing a doctor soon is important." He had at first typed imperative before changing the word to important. He had already used the word once and didn't want to spook Buzz or Dolly into doing something rash.

Instead of waiting for a reply, he left his hotel room and returned to Deer's hotel room with her key card in hand. He inserted the card into the slot on the door before he saw the tool marks on the side of the frame. The small green light came on, and the lock clicked off.

"Damn," Clint whispered to himself and made a quick decision to continue into the room. Best to act ignorant, he thought, no one knew or expected him. He entered without making another sound. The room looked the same as when he left it. He started to relax and let the door close, but before the door clicked shut, he sensed movement behind him.

Clint took a quick step to the side and spun in time to deflect the small blade of a knife intended for his back. The knife flew out of his attacker's hand, but the man continued his assault.

His assailant gave up ten inches in height and at least sixty pounds in weight, but he came at Clint without an ounce of fear. After he parried Clint's first two attempts to hit him, Clint realized he was in for a real fight. His attacker's foot flashed in front of Clint's chin, missing it by a millimeter or two and more because of Clint's size than his reaction.

Clint reached for the foot but missed. The man followed up with a short strike with his fist intended for Clint's solar plexus. Clint managed to twist enough to take the blow on his ribs. At the same time, he drove his own fist into the side of the man's head hitting him in his right temple. The man staggered back a step, and Clint followed up with a hard right into the man's left temple. His attacker went down, his chin hitting hard on the carpet.

Before the man hit the floor, another person landed on Clint's back and immediately had him in a choke hold. Clint tried two quick counter moves to break the man's hold without success. This attacker, like the last one, knew what he was doing. Clint slammed his elbow into the man's side, but the man didn't even grunt. The strike with the elbow meant to hurt more than dislodge the man, although that would have been nice. As his second attacker adjusted his position in anticipation of another elbow, Clint drew his knife out of a pocket and jammed the blade into the man's arm. He did his best to slice the man's arm all the way to the elbow.

The man screamed and let go of Clint, but Clint kept a grip on the man's arm and continued his slicing. The man worked his way in front of Clint and grabbed at the knife with his free hand. More out of instinct than strategy, Clint slammed his forehead into his assailants' face. His attacker staggered backwards and Clint's knife fell to the floor. Free from the choke hold, Clint sucked in air, and oxygen rich blood once again circulated through his brain. He saw the man reach around to his back and assumed he was reaching for a weapon of some kind. He charged the man and grabbed the hand that emerged with a small pistol. Clint smashed his free open palm into the man's nose driving the man's head back as far as he could. His assailant's knees buckled, but he kept a tight grip on the weapon.

Clint spun him around and twisted the man's arm up behind him until he heard the shoulder pop. The man gasped, and the pistol dropped out of his hand. Clint struck him hard at the base of the neck, and the man fell.

He studied the situation and looked at the time. He had been there less than two minutes. It seemed like an hour. He knew both men on the ground were still alive. He contemplated killing them, but he didn't need the police swarming the hotel. These men weren't South Korean cops. They would have identified themselves if they were. No, these two had come from North Korea and somehow had followed Deer to the hotel.

Clint noticed a small backpack on the floor by the door. Deer had brought hers with her to his room. He looked in it and found various items one might need to restrain and control someone else. The two had intended to use the items on Deer. Clint made quick use of the flex cuffs, locking both attackers' hands behind them. He rifled through their pockets but came out with very little other than wallets that had nothing in them but identity cards that were most likely fraudulent. He removed a pistol from one man and picked the other up off the floor. Both men started showing signs of regaining consciousness.

He had seen an item that could be used as a gag in the backpack. He retrieved it and put it on one of the men. Satisfied with it, Clint grabbed a hand towel from the bathroom and made a make shift gag that he used on the second man. He removed their belts and used them to fasten each man's ankles together.

Not knowing if someone else might be coming to join these two, or if they were supposed to report by phone to someone periodically, Clint felt it unwise to stay in the room much longer. He did a quick search of the room and packed everything he could find that looked like it belonged to Deer. He found a few items but not many. Deer had only partially unpacked the small suitcase. He put the men's wallets in the suitcase along with the two pistols.

He thought about photographing the two before he left but decided against it. He had spent long enough in the room. After taking one last quick glance around, Clint left and made sure the door was locked behind him.

CHAPTER 11

"She wasn't there," Kim said.

"What? Where could she have gone?" Yi asked.

"She may be in the hotel's bar or visiting someone in another room. It is her room, and her stuff is still there. She'll return at some point tonight or in the morning."

"Damn! We're running out of time!"

"I know. I left Oh and Choi in the room. I thought it would be better if I informed you of our status in person."

"You did right," Yi said while he tried to calm his racing heart and throbbing head. He took a few deep breaths before speaking again. "Those two won't have any trouble subduing one American woman."

"There was a bloody towel in the room. I think the woman is injured."

"That's good. It should slow her down."

"What do you want me to do?" Kim asked.

"Right now, let's go over what we know of the American president's itinerary. If we don't get the information that Whatley had for us, we will still have to accomplish our mission. I want to verify who on our team made it here to Busan and what weapons we have to use. I know what we planned, but I want to ensure everyone and everything we need is here."

For the next twenty minutes, the two made calls and annotated a map of Busan with the anticipated routes the president would be taking during his visit. It would not be easy, but even without Whatley's information, Yi and Kim came up with two possible ways they could eliminate their target.

"Something's wrong," Kim said.

"What?" Yi said.

"Oh was supposed to contact me ten minutes ago. When he didn't, I tried to call him. I got no answer. I need to go back in there and see what's going on."

"Want someone with you?" Yi asked.

"No. The night clerk saw me leave. My return won't be suspicious, but it might be if others are with me."

Yi nodded. "Let me know your status as soon as you get into the room."

"I will," Kim said and left. It only took him a few minutes to reach the hotel. His entrance seemed to go unnoticed. When the elevator stopped, Kim kept his head down and stepped passed a tall westerner, an American he thought, who stepped into the elevator.

Kim stopped and listened outside the hotel room. He heard nothing. He tapped on the door and waited. He glanced at the room number. Something was indeed wrong. For a second time that night, Kim popped the door open and entered in a crouch with his pistol in hand. The room was dark, but the light from the hall disclosed two figures on the floor. One of the two started moving.

He shut the door before turning on the room lights. After a quick inspection of the room and ignoring the two men on the floor, he telephoned Yi and reported his status. Only then did he free the two and help them onto the small sofa.

"What the hell happened?"

"A man, a big man," Oh mumbled. Kim could tell something had happened to Oh's jaw. He had trouble talking.

Kim looked at Choi. His right arm was soaked in blood, but he seemed to favor his left shoulder. Kim could see he was in a lot of pain. Choi's nose had bled all over his upper lip and left side of his face, but the nose bleeding had stopped. "He had a key. I was in the bathroom and didn't hear him enter. First I heard was when Oh started fighting him."

"The two of you couldn't take him?"

Choi looked down at the carpet.

"He was a professional, and he was big. I may have cut him," Oh said, although he knew he hadn't.

Kim shook his head. "He came alone? The woman didn't come with him?"

The two mumbled that he came alone.

Despite his frustration, Kim did what he could for the two men. What Oh needed required very little attention from Kim. Oh's jaw might have been broken, and he had been knocked out, but a professional would have to tend to his jaw at some later time.

While Oh sat on the sofa working the cobwebs out of his mind and gently rubbing his jaw, Kim popped Choi's shoulder back in place and used a bandage the team had in their pack to cover Choi's wound.

"Do we still wait here?" Choi asked.

"No. The man removed all the items that the woman had here. He has taken her somewhere else in this hotel. If she had left the hotel, we would have seen her."

"Can you describe the man?"

"I attacked him from behind," Choi said.

"Me, too," Oh said.

"Both of you had the advantage, and he still got away?"

"He had dark hair and was easily six and a half feet tall," Choi said.

Kim's mind shot to the westerner waiting for the elevator. He didn't think the man was six and a half foot tall, but he was tall with dark hair. Could he have been the man? Kim had only glanced at the man's face, but unlike the two losers in front of him, he would be able to provide Yi a description.

Despite telling the men they wouldn't be waiting in the room any longer, Kim decided he should call Yi again and confirm with him that they would be wasting their time and putting the mission in too much risk by staying in the room.

Yi answered Kim's call on the first ring. He hadn't expected a second call and hoped it would bring good news. It didn't. It only substantiated what they already believed and left him more depressed and irritable the he had been earlier. However, he knew Kim was right, there was no use leaving anyone in the room.

Kim sent Oh and Choi out of the hotel room first while he took one last look around. The blood on the carpet was obvious and could draw a lot of attention to the room. While the room belonged to the American woman, hotel cameras might link their presence to the room. He could think of no permanent solution, so he settled on placing the "Do Not Disturb" sign on the door. If it kept the staff out for a day or two, it would be sufficient.

"Why do you think the man didn't call the police?" Yi asked Kim after the man had returned.

"I've wondered about that, too. They don't want the police to be aware of their presence, but why?"

"Perhaps the killing of Whatley was not coordinated with Seoul."

"But they're in Busan now and far away from all that. The American's could surely come up with some false story that their puppets here would accept," Kim said.

"Could it be that a criminal organization had Whatley killed for reasons that have nothing to do with his cooperation with us?"

"But then why take the information he had for us?"

"If he had any information with him," Yi said. "We were told he had the information written for us, but maybe he didn't, or maybe he had it somewhere else."

"Damn, we're screwed," Kim said.

Ironically, his comment made Yi smile. "Wouldn't be the first time."

They both laughed before agreeing that their best course of action would be to keep the hotel under surveillance. They would grab either the man or the woman when they left and get the information. At the same time, they would work on their own assassination scenario to use in case they weren't able to retrieve Whatley's information.

Later, the two shared a bottle of soju, Korea's most popular alcoholic beverage, late into the early morning hours.

CHAPTER 12

Clint found Deer asleep when he returned to the room. He closed the bedroom door and stretched out on the large recliner chair before sending a text to Buzz updating him on their situation. He felt safe in the room but still made sure the safety locks on the inside of the hotel room door were secure. He studied one of the pistols he had taken from his assailants. A modified CZ82, a North Korean favorite, it would have to do. At least now they were armed. He checked to make sure the weapon was loaded, rested it on his lap, and closed his eyes.

Half way across the globe, Buzz read the mid-morning text and shared it with Dolly. "They're North Koreans for sure. Clint's correct. I think it's time we start doing some behind the scenes support."

"You mean more than just sitting here with our thumbs up our asses," Dolly said.

"You don't need to be so blunt, but yes," Buzz liked Dolly but thought she could be a little too crude on occasion.

Dolly thought Buzz to be a little prudish, but she liked her co-worker. She also enjoyed making him uncomfortable.

Buzz tapped his pen on a blank paper tablet like he was studying words that weren't there. "Here are my thoughts. First, we send a message to one of our friends over in NSA alerting him to our suspicions that the dead bodies found around Pyongtek were part of a team sent to the south to disrupt the president's visit to Busan. I think if we also say we are concerned they might be involved in a larger and more nefarious plot, that wouldn't be out of line for us. Second, let's send in an anonymous tip or two to the Busan police and to the Korean National Security Service like we're some anonymous Busan resident claiming we heard three men huddling at a restaurant speaking in a North Korean accent."

Dolly nodded, "They are already at a high-level alert, but I guess it can't hurt. Do we trust our translation software enough to make our anonymous tip, an email, right, seem authentic?"

"I think so, but even if they are suspicious, I think they'll still run with it. We'll identify the restaurant as one being close to the hotel."

"Hopefully, the same people who sent Deer over there are doing these same things."

"I assume they are," Buzz said, "but you know what assuming does. I'd rather have us doing something unnecessary than doing nothing right now."

Dolly nodded. "What more can we do in direct support of Deer?"

"I don't know. They'll be moving and reacting to things as they happen, and we can't anticipate those. Can you call Freda in? I think we can use an extra hand. She can support what's developing down in Venezuela."

"Sure," Dolly said. Freda had worked full time with them for seven years, but had gone to part time when she hit her mid-sixties. For the last four years she came in when needed, but otherwise stayed home.

In their cover role as a multi-disciplinary threat analysis branch situated in the bowels of the U.S. Marshal Service, Deer's headquarters staff routinely sent out threat assessments and search requests to other components within the intelligence community. This gave them significant access to intelligence and sufficient cover to network with individuals throughout the community.

"I know we're working off the theory that Deer killed the men outside Pyongtek and that other than the one American, the rest were North Koreans, but what's our theory for the North Koreans pursuing her to Busan," Dolly asked while she worked on a text message to Freda.

"I haven't figured that one out," he said and returned to his desk and started working.

Several thousand miles away, Clint heard a noise outside the hotel room and sat up. He heard voices and a door click shut. The voices moved down the hall away from his room. He glanced at his watch, four o'clock in the morning. Who would get up at this awful hour?

He peeked into the bedroom and saw that Deer was still asleep. Good for her, he thought. For the first time since his confrontation with the two men, Clint realized his ribs ached where one of the attackers struck him. He rubbed the area and did some stretches until he was sure nothing was broken. Returning to the recliner, he set the alarm on his phone for six and closed his eyes.

Sleep came in small intermittent pieces. Jet lag, more than the day's excitement, caused him to keep waking up. He forced his eyes to stay shut knowing he needed the sleep despite his body telling him that it was the middle of the afternoon back on South Padre Island, Texas.

Clint had done a lot of traveling in his life, first in the military and now in his role as a hunter. He had heard many opinions whether jet lag was harder on a person traveling east or on someone traveling west. Clint held the opinion it depended on the person, because it affected him the same no matter which way he travelled.

The sound of a toilet flushing snapped him out of his haze. He stood up and knocked gently on the bedroom door. When no one answered, he opened it and peered in. Deer had gotten out of bed, and he could hear the water running in the bathroom sink.

"How are you doing this morning?" he asked through the closed bathroom door.

The door opened and Deer walked out. "About the same. My arm and head ache, but I'll live another day." She had slipped on a long-sleeved sweatshirt at some point during the night, so Clint couldn't see how the bandage on her arm had held up.

"Besides getting out of here, what's the plan for today?" Clint asked.

"We need to pass the contents of the note that Whatley had for the North Korean contacts to the Secret Service advance team here in Busan. We may have to do it through the consulate. I connected to a secure server back home and dug up as much as I could about the team over here at the consulate. Unfortunately, what I couldn't get was a cell phone number for any of the team members already here."

Clint had started making coffee in the small one cup brewer provided by the hotel. "Want a cup?"

Deer nodded, "A lot of sugar and creamer, if you don't mind. I need it today."

Clint knew she normally drank her coffee black without anything added. "So how do we make contact?"

"Since they don't know about you, I'll need you to take the memo-"

"Hold that thought," Clint interrupted, knowing the "they" Deer referred to were the North Koreans, and relayed the events as they unfolded the night before after Deer had fallen asleep.

"I'm glad you didn't kill them in my room, but this is no good either. Think they'll recognize you when you leave?"

"I'm sure they will, but I think I can get past them. My concern is getting back to this room without their discovering which room we're in. I wouldn't put it past them to come at us in the room, and I'm sure they'll have us seriously outgunned."

"Considering neither of us is armed."

"It's not that bad," Clint said. "I lifted the pistols from the two men who attacked me last night. No extra ammo but they're both loaded."

"I bet those two are a little bit mad at you today."

Clint nodded. "I imagine they are. So, what do I do with the scribbling on that tablet?"

"I'll get to that, first though does this place have room service?" Deer asked. "I'm starving, but I think we ought to order in."

Clint located the hotel brochure and after glancing at it, handed it to Deer.

"Eggs, sausage, toast and coffee?" she asked. "They serve American."

"Fine with me. I wonder what kind of sausage we'll get."

"Who knows? Your room, want to make the call?"

"Yeah," Clint said. He picked up the room phone and ordered their breakfast.

"Your turn in the bathroom, if you want to freshen up before the food arrives."

"I think I will," Clint said and after grabbing a couple of items of clothing entered the bathroom.

"So, how do we make contact?" Clint asked about twenty minutes later as he poked at what was left of his fried egg. The white of the egg looked like it should have stayed another minute on the grill. He never liked to see fluid running out of the white when he cut into it. He pushed the runny part of the egg white off to the side of his plate.

"Other than avoiding our pursuers, it shouldn't be too hard. There's a mid-level diplomat with the consulate, a Johnny Davenport. His father served in the State Department and spent a lot of time in Korea. The father married a Korean woman, and Johnny grew up fluent in both languages. He's attending an opening of a city park today at ten. I want you to attend that ceremony. It's outdoors and open to the public. While you're there, give the tablet with Whatley's message to him. Make Davenport understand this information may have been provided to a team of North Korean assassins."

"Any suggestions how I should handle that?" Clint knew he

could come up with some ruse, but he was interested in any advice Deer might have.

"I would say that you got it from your wife who works at a restaurant and overheard four men at a table talking about assassinating the president. She wrote down what she remembered and asked you to give it to the Secret Service. Claim that she is terrified and doesn't want anyone to know about her. Tell Davenport you think the information is real and needs to be passed on to the Secret Service immediately."

"Sounds like a good plan," Clint said.

"Here's a picture of him." Deer handed him her phone. "Handsome guy."

"You want to take him the memo?"

"Twenty years ago, I might have, but not with a bruised face and all shot up. I couldn't even handle a hug today."

"I'll leave early enough to give me time to shake these guys before I rendezvous with Davenport."

"I have an idea for that," Deer said. She reached into her wallet and pulled out the card her taxi driver had given her.

Forty-five minutes later, Clint took the elevator down to the third floor and the stairs down from there. The stairs led him to a short hallway on the ground floor near a side exit. A handful of hotel offices and storage closets lined the hall which intersected at one end with a larger hall that ran from the reception area to the restaurant and bar. At the end closer to Clint, stood a door that led outside the hotel to a side street.

Clint cracked the door and looked out. A cab sat at the curb. Without hesitating, Clint opened the door and walked to the cab.

CHAPTER 13

"A cab has parked by the side door," Li Chang reported.

"Go to it and wait by the side door. If the woman comes out, force her into the cab as we planned and bring her here. Kill the driver in this lot and bring her in. If a tall, dark haired American comes out of the hotel stall him as long as you can. Another team is coming your way," Yi said.

Yi turned to the three men who had stood when they heard his conversation. "Go, now, you know where Li was posted."

The men left. Yi preferred to use two rather than three men on a team, but he needed Oh's eyes, and he knew Oh wasn't anywhere near one hundred percent yet.

When Oh and the others pulled their old Kia to a stop next to Li Chang, the man was standing by himself.

"What happened?" Oh demanded. His face displayed more pain from talking than disappointment in not having a chance to take on the big American again.

"He came straight out to the taxi, and they sped off before I could stop them. You just missed it. They turned right onto that street. With the heavy traffic, I bet it hasn't gotten far. I wrote down the number and cab line." Li thrust a piece of paper into Oh's hand.

Oh, sitting behind the driver, hit the back of the driver's seat with his hand. "Go!"

The Kia dashed away, leaving Li alone on the street. He looked around for a closer spot from which he could watch the door and still remain inconspicuous. He didn't see one, but he couldn't lose a second person, be it the woman or the man again, because he was too slow in responding. If he did, Yi would have him transferred to the rice fields picking rice for a living. He thought about Kim and shuddered. Fail Kim twice, and he might slit your throat.

Li decided to wait at a spot a few steps from the door. He leaned against the wall to the hotel. He would tell anyone suspicious of his presence there that he was waiting for a lady friend who worked in the hotel. One couldn't enter the hotel through this side door unless she had a key or knew the code. If Li could get in he might find a better place inside, but for now, the wall would have to get used to him leaning against it.

Li's mind soon moved to a topic that he knew he shouldn't dwell on, but he couldn't help it. He had only been outside North Korea on a few missions. Twice those trips took him to Iran where he didn't have these thoughts. However, this was his second mission into South Korea, and like the last mission, he couldn't help but wonder how much better it would be to live in a place like Busan or Seoul, than back in the north.

He never spoke of his thoughts. Doing so could put him in jail. At a minimum, he would not be allowed to leave North Korea again, and he needed to be able to leave. Some day in the future he knew he would stay gone. Not now, and preferably not so close to Pyongyang, but he knew of a half-dozen locations where the tentacles of his own security agency had a hard time reaching.

Li Chang stared at a young woman as she hurried by him on the other side of the street. She paid him no attention, but he couldn't keep his eyes off her. The way she dressed, the way she carried herself, and her good looks reinforced Li's belief that he shouldn't wait until he was an old man to disappear.

Li looked up at the intersection, but the car with the team of North Korean assassins had already disappeared around the corner.

For its part, after forcing its way around the corner, the car with the North Korean team of assassins made it through the first traffic light it encountered as the light turned red when the car passed underneath.

"There it is. Fortune is with us," Oh said from the back seat.

"I've got it," the driver replied.

A block ahead and separated by at least eight or nine cars, the taxi crept north among the hoard of cars that filled the street. Oh Chung Chin considered jumping out of the car and jogging up the sidewalk. With this traffic, he would have a good chance of catching up with the taxi before the car he now sat in would. However, the pain in his jaw reminded him that jogging in his condition would not be an enjoyable activity, and he would look the fool if the taxi made a sudden turn and drove down a less congested side street.

Yi had ordered them to kill the big American and then search him, rather than to try to capture him. This had pleased Oh. He didn't want to get within arm's length of the American, but he would find putting a few slugs into the man's gut very fulfilling.

They followed the taxi for nearly a mile making very little progress in closing the gap between the two cars. When the taxi finally turned off the busy street, Oh thought they would lose it. Despite the short distance, it took nearly a minute for the Kia to take the same turn. For the next couple of minutes, the taxi was nowhere in sight. They continued down the street looking back and forth down all intersections.

"There it is," the driver said and pointed at a taxi trying to return to the street from a driveway that led into a small outdoor park.

As they approached it, the taxi pulled out onto the street and drove past them.

"He wasn't in the taxi," Oh said. "He must have gotten out. Turn in here."

The driver made a quick turn barely avoiding a white sedan coming from the other direction. The sedan's driver honked at them but drove on.

The driveway ended in a parking lot to what looked like a

park or a small green space surrounded by large buildings. The driver located the only spot free and parked the Kia in it. They watched the small crowd gathered in the park about thirty yards away.

"Not a good place to do anything. Too many people, only one way out, and two policemen are right over there," Oh said.

The other two men in the car remained silent. Oh wondered if they'd be happy to sit in the car and do nothing for the rest of the day. Not everyone had the motivation of Yi or Kim. He scrutinized the crowd. The American should be easy to find as he should tower over everyone. Where was he? There were a few Americans spread out in the gathering, but none were the tall man with the black hair.

"There he is!" Oh almost shouted and his jaw immediately reminded him that it wasn't a good idea to shout.

"Where?" the two men in the front seats asked simultaneously.

"A little away from the crowd, leaning against that tree."

The two had to look at Oh to see at which tree he was pointing. They followed his finger to the man.

"Are you sure? He looks relaxed, like he doesn't have a care in the world," the driver said.

"That's him, and don't let him fool you. He's a professional," Oh rubbed his jaw. "We stay close to him, and when he's away from this crowd we take him out."

"What do we do if he's with someone?" the third assassin in the car asked.

"Same thing we would have done to the taxi driver. We kill them, too," Oh said. "We can't have any witnesses, and don't forget, we have to check him for any documents."

Oh wondered what the American was doing. A small park's grand opening in the middle of Busan didn't seem like something where an American operative would be wasting his time. He didn't appear to have any part in the ceremony.

Three separate speakers talked for the next thirty-five minutes about the new park and what it meant for this part of the city. Oh had his window down and listened but had little interest. They had missed the beginning of the ceremony, so Oh had no idea who the dignitaries were, who the speakers were or the identities of anyone else in attendance. All three of the speakers expressed appreciation to an American group that helped fund the park. Oh looked around and didn't see anything that would have cost that much: two playgrounds for children, a pavilion, some walking paths, and a bunch of trees and flowers. Still, Oh thought, it was a nice park.

When the speakers stopped talking, the crowd started to disperse. A few left, but most of them drifted toward a couple of tables set up off to the side for food and drinks. Oh could tell he was getting hungry, but the thought of chewing anything with his jaw like it was kept thoughts of eating at bay. Two days, he thought. One way or the other the mission would be over in two days, and he would see a doctor about his jaw.

"He's finally moving," the driver said.

They watched as the American strolled over to the crowd. He stopped and appeared to be in conversation with a woman.

Oh got out of the car but stayed close to it. He motioned to the other two to stay in the vehicle. He had gotten out to better watch the American. He needed to see if the man passed anything to one of the attendees. That would complicate things. They only had one car which made following two people difficult. The American laughed at something the woman said. The woman didn't look Korean, and Oh thought she was extremely attractive. Perhaps a girlfriend, but no, neither made any attempt to touch the other. The American kept glancing over at a small group in conversation near the tables with the refreshments. The woman looked that way, and the two turned their bodies toward the small group.

"What's happening?" the driver asked through his open

window.

"Nothing yet."

Finally, the American and the woman parted ways, and the man started following another man leaving the ceremony. As the two neared a car in the parking lot, they stopped and started talking. A third man stood next to the car. Only a short distance away, Oh could almost hear their voices. The urge to make his move was almost irresistible, but Oh did the prudent thing and returned to the car. He didn't need the American to recognize him. During the dedication ceremony, the American seemed to be absorbed in watching the activities. He never turned and looked directly at Oh, but the American had been wearing sunglasses, and Oh couldn't be sure what he had seen.

Oh watched as the two men and the driver got into the large black Hyundai.

"Stay close to that car and stop it as soon as possible once we get away from here," Oh said.

A number of cars were leaving the park, but they managed to position themselves right behind the black sedan in the line of cars waiting to get back out onto the road. Oh noticed diplomatic tags on the sedan.

"Think we're being a little too obvious?" the driver said.

"Three men in an old car leaving the ceremony, I doubt it," Oh said. "Let's get ready. If they turn back to the right, there's a small, empty parking lot belonging to a church. We drove by it when we came here. Cut them off there. Once we get them off the street, I'll take out the driver so they won't be going anywhere else."

The driver grunted an acknowledgement. "You need to get that jaw fixed. It's making you hard to understand."

"I know it. Stay close to the car."

They watched their prey make a right turn, and in another thirty seconds they made their move. Their small car darted ahead of the shiny black sedan and forced it off the road into the parking lot. The three assassins jumped out of their car. Oh fired three quick times at the driver. He watched the glass in the window shatter and the man's head rock violently as the rounds hit their target.

CHAPTER 14

Earlier, when Clint opened the side door to the hotel and peered out, he saw a taxi parked next to the curb only a few feet away. The driver had his window open and watched Clint walk out the door.

"Ted, I think you're here to pick me up," Clint said, opening the door to the cab and climbing into the back seat.

"I sure am. Where would you like to go?"

Clint gave him the name of the park where he expected to find Davenport.

"The new one, where the grand opening is today?" Ted asked and drove the taxi away from the curb.

"That's it," Clint said. "You know about it?"

He glanced out the back window and saw a lone man hustling up the street toward them. He stopped as the taxi drove off, but Clint got a good look at his face. He could see disappointment and what looked like a weapon in the man's left hand.

"The service has a webpage listing all the significant events in the city each day. It helps us stay a little ahead of the game."

"Makes sense."

"How's Michelle doing? She looked like she might be coming down with something yesterday."

Clint knew he was referring to Deer. She identified herself as Michelle on the phone earlier in the morning when she called Ted to schedule the pickup. She had told Ted to expect a man and not her. She also said the man would be using the side door because he didn't want to be seen coming out of the hotel.

"I'm trying to talk her into seeing a doctor but she's stubborn. Claims she'll be okay in another day or two."

The taxi made a right turn at the intersection. Clint glanced back again and saw the man who had hurried up the street after them now standing by the hotel's side door. So far, so good, he thought.

"Well, I hope she'll be okay. She seemed like a nice lady," Ted said. He also wondered why his passenger hadn't wanted to be seen leaving the hotel. A secret lover? Most likely, he thought. In his job, he had encountered hundreds of them. He knew it was the dumb man who drove his own car to rendezvous with his mistress.

"She is, but like I said, stubborn."

The taxi crawled along in the heavy Busan traffic. Clint had given himself plenty of time, but the slow pace soon had him worrying if he should have left earlier.

"On the weekends, the traffic isn't this bad," Ted said. He honked at a jay walker who had stopped in front of the taxi and now waited for the car next to the taxi to move forward enough to let him cross into the next lane.

"Are you in the military?" Ted asked.

"I was for a while, but not anymore."

"Ever assigned over here?"

"No, been here once or twice, but never for more than a couple days."

"It takes a while for most Americans to get used to it, but most end up liking it here once they do."

"I think that's how it is in most places," Clint said.

"Tomorrow it may be impossible to get around Busan. You know the president is arriving for a two-day visit."

"I've heard about that. Why come here rather than Seoul?"

"It's a symbolic gesture of the United States continued support for Korea's freedom and democracy. It goes back to the war when what was left of the Korean army was driven back to a small area around Busan. With the assistance of the Americans and a few other allies, they held this small patch of the country and eventually drove the invaders back up north. I think it's a symbolic gesture for the rest of the Asian Pacific rim on how the U.S. is prepared to support South Korea and everyone else against Chinese aggression."

"You stay on top of current events," Clint said.

"It's been on the news a lot lately. I hope to be able to attend one of the events open to the public. I know a lot of people are protesting the visit, but the President of the United States is visiting our city, and I think that's great. Besides, I've never actually seen one in person before."

"Neither have I," Clint said.

"Are you involved in the park's opening celebration this morning?"

"No. I'm meeting someone there."

"Want me to wait for you?"

"Thanks, but I hope to get a lift back with my friend." Clint wasn't sure how things would work out, but he didn't want to put this young cab driver in danger. He didn't know if he was being tailed, but it wouldn't surprise him if somewhere behind them among the dozens of cars was a North Korean killer or two. He knew they wouldn't hesitate to kill him and anyone else with him.

"We should be there in just another minute," Ted said after turning off the main street onto a two-lane road busy with traffic but moving along at a good pace.

Clint watched the road behind him and saw a few vehicles also make the turn, but he didn't sense that any of them were following him. When they turned into the park entrance, he watched again for a car to pull in behind them or slow down as they passed the park. None did.

"Thanks, Ted. Could I have your card, too? Michelle has the one you gave her, and if you don't mind, I may have a need later today for a ride."

"Sure," Ted said. He could always use the business, and both

Michelle yesterday and this man today were great tippers. "I can wait."

"No, I'm good but thanks," Clint said and walked off to the side of the gathering.

He watched the taxi head up the driveway to the stop sign before he turned his attention to the crowd. According to what Deer had told him, Davenport should be in attendance representing the consulate. Clint could see that all the seats set up for the ceremony were occupied, and ten to fifteen people stood behind those seated. For the moment, everyone listened to the speaker, a young woman. She stopped speaking shortly after Clint's arrival, and the audience gave a brief applause. An old man rose form one of the chairs in the front row and took the podium. Like the woman, he spoke in Hangul, the local language, and Clint had no idea what they were saying.

Clint moved to the side of the group and leaned against a large tree. His new position gave him a better vantage point from which he could look for Davenport, but he still couldn't pick him out. Three men who looked like they could be Americans sat in the front row, but Clint knew he would have to wait until the ceremony ended to locate and approach Davenport.

He noticed another car drive into the parking lot but didn't pay it too much attention.

Two young women removed a paper sheet from the top of a table across from where Clint stood exposing a variety of refreshments. Shortly after that, the speaker stopped talking, the crowd applauded, and the official part of the ceremony appeared to come to an end. Clint knew that several people would stick around for the refreshments and to visit with other attendees, but he didn't know if Davenport would stay or make a beeline for his car.

A slight gust of wind blew a few napkins off a table and caused a number of people to look up at the sky. That's when

Clint saw him. One of the young women who had been standing by the refreshment table approached Davenport and offered him a cup of coffee or tea. He accepted the cup and began talking to two Korean men next to him.

"Did you enjoy the ceremony?"

Clint turned his attention to the attractive woman dressed in a dark blue pants suit. "I'm not good with the language," he said. "I came because I need to speak to Mr. Davenport, but it seems like the audience enjoyed it."

"Most of them have spent a long time making this park a reality. There are too few good parks where children can play."

"From what I can see, it's a lovely park. I'm Maxwell Steel, by the way, nice to meet you," Clint held out his hand.

"I'm Eleanor Rivers," she said taking his hand. "You must not be from here, or I would have met you long ago." She smiled, and Clint knew she was flirting.

"Just here for a few days. What brings you here today?"

"I'm a member of the Chamber of Commerce, or the equivalent of what we have in America. The Chamber helped donate funds as did my church. I've been a big advocate, so I felt obliged to come to the opening."

"How long have you lived here in Busan?" Clint asked. He might as well talk to this woman, since Davenport appeared to be engrossed in his own conversation.

"Twelve years. My husband and I came over here with his job. He did quite well, grew the business, and for the last six years of his life ran the Asian Pacific operations."

"Last six years?" Clint asked.

"He died eighteen months ago. A bad stroke. It happened instantly. They say he worked too hard, but I think it was caused by his refusal to stop smoking. Everybody still smokes here in Korea."

"Sorry."

"It took a while to get over it, as much as one can that is. I would've gone home, but the company asked me to stay on for a year as a way to help the new boss break into all the right circles. No official title, of course, but the pay was ridiculously high."

"No longer employed?"

"Not in any real sense. They have me on retainer, so I still make an appearance now and then. I keep thinking I'll head back, but then I can't decide where to head back to. Besides, I've got a lot of friends in Busan and have my fingers in more projects than I should."

"Keeps you busy."

"What brings you to Korea?" she asked.

"Business, part of an Asian trip."

She looked at him wanting to know more but decided not to ask. He kept glancing at Davenport, so she shifted her stance and gaze to make it easier for both of them to keep an eye on him.

"Is he expecting you?"

"No. That's why I'll need to grab him before he leaves."

"He's a nice man, has a nice wife. I'm surprised she's not here today. She had a hand in this project. Do you know her?"

"No. Don't really know him. Maybe next trip, if I can make it a longer visit, I'll get a chance to meet her. In fact, if I can get back here, I may even need an escort to show me around the city," Clint said and smiled at Rivers. He guessed she might be ten years or so older than him, but she looked great. He noticed that a number of the Korean men in the audience would frequently look in her direction. He didn't blame them.

She smiled in return. "I would like that. I can be a pretty good tour guide. You better get going. I think Johnny is making his move."

"Yeah, I should go."

"Here," she offered Clint a business card. "I'm having a small party at the house this evening. If you're free, Maxwell, give me a call, I'll send a driver around to get you."

"Thanks, I hope I can," he took her card and walked after

Assistant Consular Johnny Davenport.

As Davenport approached the parking lot, a man joined him. The way the man simply nodded at Davenport as he came up alongside him indicated to Clint that he was most likely Davenport's driver.

"Mr. Davenport," Clint said.

The diplomat barely broke stride as he looked back. "Sir, I need to get to a meeting, so please be quick."

"I only need a couple minutes of your time."

The driver said something to Davenport.

"Can you give this number a call, and I'll try to give you some time as soon as I can." Like Ms. Rivers had done a minute before, Davenport held out a business card for Clint to take.

They had reached the car and the driver held the back door open for Davenport. He started to slide in.

"It's about the president's visit. It's very important. Let me ride with you, and I can tell you everything before we get to the consulate. I don't know who else to go to or how to contact anyone else."

"This should go to the Secret Service, not to me."

"Agreed, but I don't know how to do that. You do."

"Okay, hop in," Davenport said. Clint could tell from his tone that he wasn't thrilled with Clint getting in his car. He also noticed the driver now looking at him with a hint of a threat in his eyes.

Clint hurried around the car and got in the back seat next to Davenport.

"Thanks, Johnny."

"Do I know you?"

"No, but that doesn't matter. What I have to pass on to you is very, very important. I need you to take this and give it immediately to the Secret Service contingent that's here in advance of the President's arrival." Clint offered the small memo pad, but Davenport looked at it as though it might be contagious.

"I don't read Hangul, but I believe it's information that may have been provided to someone who intends to assassinate the president. Read it, I might be wrong."

The car turned right and started picking up speed on the street. Davenport took the memo pad and started reading the message. "What is this about?"

"What does it say?"

"It's a note simply giving a location here in Busan and a vantage point to best view it. Wait a second. This is one of his stops. Where did you get this?"

"It's not important. A Korean friend of mine, who is terrified about getting involved, picked it up from where it had been accidently dropped on the floor by a group of men. She said they spoke with a northern accent. She got the impression they were talking about the president's visit."

"Doesn't mean they want to assassinate him," Davenport said.

"I know, but it won't hurt to pass this on to the Secret Service along with my friend's concerns. Will you do that?"

"Sure, but I need to know who you are, and I think it would be better if you..." Davenport was interrupted by a white car speeding around and in front of Davenport's car and forcing them to make a sudden turn into an adjacent parking lot.

"Go! Don't stop!" Clint shouted, but the startled driver stopped the car in the empty parking lot despite the warning.

Before the driver could get the car moving again, the sound of gunshots exploded from a few feet away, and Clint could see the driver's head jerk to his right.

"Down!" Clint shouted to Davenport while he opened the car door and rolled out. He didn't look to see if Davenport ducked or not.

More gunfire erupted. Clint stood and using the trunk of the sedan as cover returned fire. He saw two men shooting while they climbed out of the Kia and the third firing through an open window. Clint fired without hesitation. One, two, three and repeat. One, two, three. Six shots in three seconds and at this close range none of Clint's shots deviated more than an inch from his targets.

He knew it would be prudent to check the men he shot, but he also knew he had hit them all in vital areas. He turned his attention to Davenport who lay on the floor of the car. He could see blood spreading on the shoulder of Davenport's suit.

"Johnny, are you okay?"

Rather than say anything, Davenport looked up. His face pale, when he tried to speak his voice came out in high toned gasps.

"Sit up, it's over. Look at me," Clint ordered.

Davenport struggled to get back into his seat but managed to do so. He didn't seem to realize that he had been shot.

"I have to go," Clint said.

"You can't go now," Davenport gasped. He hadn't yet looked around.

"Listen to me. It's critical you get that note to the Secret Service."

Davenport looked at his hand where the memo pad had been squeezed into a wad but was still there.

"The men who attacked us are from North Korea. The police will be able to verify that. They are killers. I cannot stay; I still have work to do. Can you understand that?"

For the first time, Davenport looked around and nodded. Clint did not see him nod as he was already moving to the Kia. He pulled the third gunman out of the car and let him fall onto the pavement. The car's engine was still idling. Clint got into the driver's seat and after pushing it back as far as it would go, he drove the car out of the parking lot and onto the street where cars had already begun slowing down to observe what was happening.

Clint drove through three intersections before turning off the street and continuing another five blocks. He turned the car into a public parking garage and parked in the first spot he found.

After wiping the steering wheel and door handles with his handkerchief, he left the car and exited the parking garage out a side door.

Despite his black hair, he knew blending in with the local population was not an option. Very few Korean men stood over six feet tall. He needed to get as far away as he could. He could hear the police sirens all around him as he walked. Luck stayed with him as he came to an intersection with another busy street. A taxi was dropping off a fare not far from him. Clint jogged down to the taxi, and after being waved in by the driver, squeezed into the small back seat.

The driver asked Clint something in the local language.

"Do you speak English?" Clint asked.

The two stared at each other for a second. For a variety of reasons, he didn't want to take this taxi back to the hotel, but the hotel was the only place in Busan he knew by name and which he thought the driver might recognize. Then he remembered the card that the flight attendant had given him. He took it out of his wallet and showed it to the driver.

The driver looked at the card and then out the front window. He turned back to Clint and said something that Clint inferred as a reluctance to take Clint to the restaurant. Through a couple hand signals, he finally convinced the driver to take him to the restaurant. The driver said something and shook his head, but he drove the taxi away from the curb.

Clint had to laugh when the cab driver stopped in front of the restaurant only one block away from where he had jumped into it. The driver had his own grin and pointed at the adjacent restaurant. At first, the taxi driver declined payment. Clint figured the driver couldn't wait to tell all his friends about the dumb American who hired his cab to go about fifty yards. His insistence in paying the driver would at least prevent him from being called a cheap, dumb American.

CHAPTER 15

Despite the late hour, Dolly sat at her desk reading the classified intelligence reports coming in from Korea. Not interested in the lengthier final products, Dolly keyed in on spot reports and the initial raw reporting that ran almost like classified news feeds. She also had one screen monitoring the various commercial English language news headlines emanating from South Korea. The third screen kept her informed of the real time locations of Theresa Deer and Clint Smith.

"Hey, Buzz! Something's happening," she called out to Buzz who was taking a nap on a recliner in Deer's office.

"What's up," he mumbled coming out of the office still half asleep.

Dolly waited until he stood next to her and had shaken off the stupor of sleep.

"Three men tried to kill a diplomat in Busan. They got the driver but only wounded the diplomat. All three assassins were killed by a man travelling with the diplomat at the time. No ID on the man, but from the timing and Clint's location at the time, it was him. No information on whether this other man, Clint, incurred any injuries."

"This is not good," Buzz said.

"I know. The South Korean security agencies are going crazy. There is talk on the wires that the would-be assassins are from North Korea. With the president arriving in Busan, the city is being locked down as much as it's possible to lock down a city of over three million."

"How much of this is getting out in the open press?"

"Right now, very little. I mean the attempted assassination is headline news, but the North Korean connection has not yet been released.   There's been an acknowledgement that a third man was in the car with the diplomat, but no details."

"That's good. The last thing we need right now is his picture splattered all over the evening television news," Buzz said.

"Any word from either of them?"

"No, not since the short text a few hours ago."

"Their plane leaves in eight hours. I hope they're on it," Dolly said.

Buzz looked at his phone. "What in the world?"

"Clint?"

"No, but someone I need to go see."

"Now?" Dolly asked.

"Yes."   Buzz went back into Deer's office and put on his shoes. He sent Deer a quick text telling her that he had been summoned by her boss. Before he got out of the building, he received a return text from her.

"Make sure he gets this. Info provided to Johnny Davenport this morning," the text said. It also contained an internet link. Buzz clicked on the link and a few lines of what Buzz assumed was written in Hangul appeared on a plain white background. Deer provided no explanation.

Washington D.C. isn't the safest city to walk around in at night, but since the meeting place was only a block and half away, Buzz made the trip on foot. He entered the diner that he thought had once been a Denny's and looked around. Four or five men, all looking like they were part of the city's homeless sat at the counter. They weren't bunched together; one or two stools separated each of them from the others.

Only one table had customers seated at it. The oldest of the three, wearing a Georgetown University sweatshirt, waved for Buzz to join them. When Buzz approached the table, the two other men, dressed more neatly and wearing lightweight windbreakers to hide the weaponry they carried, rose from the table and moved to a spot that kept them between their charge and the men at the bar or anyone else who might enter the diner.

Thomas stood and stuck his hand out. Buzz accepted the handshake and started to speak.

"Sit down, sit down. No need for formal introductions. You know who I am or you wouldn't have come, and I know you work for Ms. Deer. Buzz, right?"

"Yes, sir." Buzz had never met Thomas before, but he had seen him, and he knew where Leon Thomas fit in the non-existent organizational chart.

"I'm sorry to bother you this late at night, but I need to know a few things before tomorrow," Thomas said.

"How can I help you?"

"I expected to hear from Deer by now."

"Has she contacted you at all?" Buzz asked.

"One short cryptic note telling me that she had accomplished the task."

"I'll tell you everything I know, sir, but I'm at a complete disadvantage since I don't know what she was supposed to do, or why, or by when."

"That's best for you. What do you know?"

"From the beginning?"

"Yes, from the beginning," Thomas said.

Buzz walked him through everything that he and Dolly knew or had surmised from the intelligence they had been able to gather.

"So she's been injured?" Thomas asked.

"Yes. She won't go to a doctor in Korea because, well, in my opinion, she'd rather die than do anything that might compromise what we do."

"This latest shootout, an hour or so ago, are you sure your man was the man with Davenport?"

"Yes, Cli-," Buzz stopped himself from saying the name.

"I don't need names," Thomas said, gesturing with his hand for Buzz to continue.

"Yes. We have pinpointed our man's movements, and he was there. I believe he was meeting Davenport to give him this." Buzz held out his phone.

Thomas glanced at the phone. "Can you read it?"

"No."

"That's probably good. Do you know where it came from?"

"No, I thought you might. Deer retrieved it from somewhere, and she thought it important enough to get it to the consulate in Busan," Buzz said.

"How do I get a copy?"

"Type this link into your phone."

Thomas did and then clicked on it. "Interesting. Can anyone reach this link?"

"If they know to look for it. URL's like this are used frequently these days for dead drops. More secure than sticking a note under a rock by a certain tree."

"What will they think of next?" Thomas said smiling. "When are you getting her out of the country?"

"Later today."

"Good, we don't want to lose her. Unfortunately, after today's incident, I believe the South Koreans will be looking for your man. Better get them both out."

"That's the plan. He went there to help Deer."

He grimaced. "That bad, huh?"

"I think so."

"Damn, that's not good."

"How badly was Davenport injured?" Buzz asked.

"Not too bad, but his driver died at the scene."

They sat there looking at each other for a minute. Buzz could see that Thomas was thinking about something.

"Ok, thanks for coming by," Thomas said.

Buzz knew he was being dismissed. He stood and left the diner. It was only after he was outside that he realized he didn't even get a cup of coffee out of the meeting. One of Thomas' bodyguards stepped outside and watched Buzz walk away. At first Buzz wondered why he was being watched, then it dawned on him that the man watched him to make sure none of the occasional thugs that roamed the empty streets of D.C. bothered him on his short walk back to his office.

Arriving at his office unmolested, Buzz found Dolly hard at work sifting through a number of computer screens.

"What's up?"

"The Secret Service is all over the shooting, and it appears Davenport has described Clint in some detail. Luckily, Clint was wearing sunglasses, but otherwise Davenport has provided a fairly good description. Right now, the Service is handling him as a good guy, but they are reaching out to other agencies to find out who he is. They also want to know what any agencies might know about the alleged, their word not mine, North Korean shooters."

"Are the South Korean police looking for him?"

"Yes. Best I can tell they don't consider him a bad guy, but they don't take kindly to any foreigner shooting anyone one on their turf."

"I figured that would happen," Buzz said.

"Davenport is giving Clint credit for saving his life and has stated that he only fired back in self-defense."

"Still, it will suck if he gets caught by anyone."

"You know, he won't say anything," Dolly said.

"I know, and how do you think that will go over with the South Koreans?"

"Probably not well. What really sucks is that no one in our government will own up to him either."

"Not right away, but I think somebody would over time."

"All this just to save a president most of the country doesn't like anyway."

"Ours is not to reason why, ours is but to do and die," Buzz said.

"At least you could come up with an original quote. You know, like life sucks and then you die," Dolly grinned.

"Oh yeah, real original. How about-" his phone interrupted him as he received a text message.

"It's Deer. She's heard about the attack on Davenport. Wants to know anything we might have learned."

"Should I ask Clint if he's okay?" Dolly asked.

"Davenport reported that he didn't think the man with him was shot, but ask away. I'll start writing my text back to Deer."

Dolly sent a short text to Clint and got an immediate "I'm okay" response back. She sent a text back to him asking him what he needed from them.

"He says he's fine," Dolly told Buzz.

A new message popped up on one of her computer screens. She had this screen set to feed her any messages sent out by the Secret Service advance team in Busan.

"Looks like some information has made it to the Secret Service team in Busan that has them really shook up."

Buzz stopped writing his text and moved around the desk to look at the screen over Dolly's shoulder.

"See this," Dolly said and pointed at a line on the screen.

"They're strongly recommending the President cancel his trip."

"Whatever information they developed, it's got them excited. At a minimum, they're suggesting he change his itinerary."

"I don't blame them. Their job is to keep the president safe, not happy. I think the information they're referring to is this." He held out his phone for Dolly to look at the picture on the screen of the note he had received from Deer.

"Looks Greek to me."

"Korean."

"How do you think Deer got her hands on that memo anyway? I don't think she can read or write Hangul," Dolly said.

"Who knows? What we do know, or at least think we know,

is that she flies to Korea on short notice, she's barely there a day or two, and she gets into a gunfight with a bunch of North Koreans. We don't know if the dead American found there was a good guy or a bad guy. She goes to Busan, and the first night she's there more North Koreans break into her room and get into it with Clint. We don't have any details on any of that, just a few remarks in texts with no explanations. We know she's seriously hurt and now hiding in Clint's room."

"Somehow they follow Clint to his meeting with Davenport and attack who? Were they after Clint or Davenport?" Dolly asked.

"Had to be after Clint, but why? It had to be they thought Clint might have something they wanted."

"Like something she found out about the North Koreans?" Dolly asked. "Maybe like what's on your screen there." Dolly nodded her head toward Buzz' phone.

"Exactly. So, their mission should be over. Accomplished."

"Okay, but can we get them out of the country?"

"Why can't they catch the plane we have them booked on today?" Buzz had already thought of a number of obstacles but wanted Dolly's take on the plan.

"Perhaps because the South Korean police will have Clint's sketch at every security checkpoint at the airport," she said.

"Exactly," Buzz repeated. "Normally, we would tell them to lay low for two to three days and get them out of Busan by car. However, with the attack on Davenport, the dead bodies found near Pyongtek, the North Korean involvement, and the president's visit, I don't see how they're going to get out of the city."

"But if they stay in Busan, it's only a matter of time before someone spots Clint and turns him in."

"Well, at least for the moment they haven't released Clint's image to the public."

"That will give him a little time, but alone without any

contacts in that city I'm not sure if he can stay hidden."

"And don't forget that Deer needs medical attention," Buzz said.

"This whole situation sucks. Can't whoever you just went to see help us out?"

"He was on the receive mode only. He didn't offer any suggestions or help. You know, though, I sensed he was concerned about her."

Dolly didn't have to ask who Buzz went to see. She couldn't remember such a meeting ever happening before, but it could only have been one person.

"What's he like?" she asked.

"Seemed like a normal guy. A normal guy with body guards."

CHAPTER 16

Clint entered the restaurant. Although the door was open, the restaurant had the appearance of being closed. The lights had not all been turned on, and one man skirted from table to table placing or rearranging items. He ignored Clint.

A text came in from Dolly, and he answered it telling her he was okay. He sent a quick text to Deer telling her the same and that he might be another hour or so getting back. While he wondered if Deer knew anything about the attack on Davenport, he didn't mention it.

"How nice, you came to my parent's restaurant." Clint looked up and saw May, the flight attendant he met briefly at the airport, walking toward him. "You're just in time. I'm having some lunch made before we get busy. Will you join me?"

"Of course, that's why I'm here."

May smiled and took Clint's hand. "Come on with me, I'm in one of our private rooms."

She led Clint out of the main dining room into a small adjacent room that had a large table centered in it. Although the table could easily seat ten people, it had been set with only one place setting.

Despite Clint not seeing May signal or say anything to anyone, a small older woman appeared within seconds with another place setting and hot tea for two. May spoke to the woman. About the only thing Clint understood was May thanking her. The woman took a step back and looked at Clint.

"You may have to help me with ordering lunch," Clint said.

"You like beef?" she asked.

"Yes."

"To drink? A beer?"

"Sounds good," Clint said. He didn't really care. He needed to kill some time for things to calm down a little outside.

"I'm very glad you came today. Please sit down. How's your stay in Busan?"

"It's been good," he sat down in the chair to her left.

"You should have brought your mother with you."

"She's not feeling that well. I think it's something she ate," Clint said. Until she mentioned his mother he had forgotten that he told May at the airport that he came to Busan to join her on vacation. "She wanted to stay at the hotel, so I decided to take advantage of your offer."

"I'm glad you did. You know, I don't even know your name," she said.

"Clint," he replied. He had traveled under his name. At that time no one had anticipated the mess he would be stepping into. "And yours is May, right?

She nodded. "How tall are you, Clint?" she smiled and reached out putting her hand on his.

For the next hour, the two of them sat there talking and eating. Clint enjoyed his lunch and told May that more than once. She worked with him on his use of chopsticks until he finally got to the point where more food reached his mouth than fell back onto his plate. When asked, he told her he worked in banking but was aspiring to become an author.

"Have you written a book?' she asked.

"Not yet, but I'm working on it."

Clint changed the topic by asking her about her life. May said she was a single mother with one son. As a flight attendant, she travelled constantly. Her parents had always taken care of her son while she was travelling, but her absence caused her ex to find someone who was willing to spend more time with him. With her ex, she clarified, not her son. Despite this, she didn't seem to hold any animosity toward her former husband.

While Clint and May had their lunch in the private room, a

lone policeman entered the restaurant, looked around and left. He sent a short text back to his headquarters stating that the tall American wasn't in the restaurant. Afterwards, the policeman continued down the block quietly inspecting every business open to the public for the American. Hundreds of other policemen and women did the same throughout this section of the city.

The Americans had stressed to the Korean police that the man with Davenport had fired in self-defense. They even had the audacity to say that time would be better spent focusing on security for the upcoming state visit than trying to track the shooter down. However, as the Director of the Korean National Police pointed out to his number two, it didn't take a rocket scientist to see something major was going on in their country between the Americans and the North Koreans. One American and a half dozen North Korean dead in a matter of days on their soil would not be something they would ignore. South Korea would make its own determination on what to focus its time and attention.

"Would you like dessert?" May asked oblivious to the large manhunt going on outside.

"No, but thanks. Everything was great."

"I need to get to work. I hope I get to see you again before you leave Busan." She put her hand on top of his. "I'm free tonight."

"Maybe tomorrow night. Can I reach you at the number you gave me?"

"Yes."

"Oh, by the way, is there a pharmacy near here? I'd like to pick up something for my mother."

"Just out our side door. Come, follow me." She took him out a side door and pointed to a shop across the street.

"Great, thanks."

"What do you want? I'll write it down for you. I don't know if they speak English," May said and took a small tablet out of her pocket.

"Something to settle her stomach and an antibiotic in case it's more than something she ate."

May scribbled a note and gave it to Clint. "I hope she gets better soon."

"I'm sure she will. Are you sure I can't pay you for the lunch?"

"No, no, it was nice to have you as my guest. I hope to see you again soon."

"I think you will," Clint said with a wink and walked away. The narrow side street allowed traffic in only one direction. Clint waited for a car to go by and jogged across to the other side.

A young man worked behind the counter while a young woman stood on the customer side. She didn't appear to be a customer as the two laughed at something they were saying, and their body language indicated they wished the counter didn't separate them.

Clint found some Tylenol, Pepto Bismal, and something he believed was an antibiotic, but he decided to use the note to be sure.

"Do you speak English?"

"My English no good," the young man answered.

The woman said something and they both laughed again. "A little," she said and pointed at the man behind the counter. She pointed at herself, "A little, too."

Clint smiled and handed the note May had given him to the young woman. She studied it and looked to see what Clint had in his basket.

"Yes," she said and pointed toward the Pepto Bismal. She picked up the Tylenol and said, "Okay." She wasn't sure about the third medicine and held it up for the pharmacist to see. She said something to him that Clint didn't understand. The man shook his head and walked over to a locked cabinet behind the counter.

"This better," he said and talked in Hangul to his lady friend.

"Better against more different bacteria or germs," she said.

"Thank you very much," Clint said and then tried to repeat the phrase in the local language. That made both of them smile.

"Good," she said.

Clint paid for the medicine, but before stepping out of the building he dialed Ted's number to see if he could pick him up in the taxi. When Ted asked him where he was, Clint had to have the young women provide Ted with the address.

"I'll be there in ten minutes," Ted said.

Clint spent the time inside a phone store and a small grocery store where he purchased a few apples. He didn't want to wait outside on the street in case the local police were driving around on the lookout for a tall, dark haired American.

He saw Ted drive up and park next to the pharmacy.

"Thanks," Clint said when he climbed into the cab.

"Thank you. Sorry it took me a little longer. Did you hear about the attempt on the diplomat this morning?"

"What? No, but people could have been talking about it all around me, and I wouldn't have understood. What happened?"

"Don't know for sure. Very little has been released on the news."

Clint wondered if Ted suspected something.

"Nothing happened at the ceremony, and I came straight here afterwards. I met a young lady whose parents own the restaurant back there. Very beautiful woman, she's a flight attendant for Korean Air."

"Oh, a flight attendant," Ted said. "Like the Navy, a man in every port." He grinned at Clint through the rear-view mirror.

"There are possibilities, but that was only our first date," he grinned back.

"Where to?"

"Back to the hotel."

"I'm going to take a few side streets to avoid the congestion,"

Ted said.

"No problem," Clint put on his sunglasses and slid down a little in the seat like he was stretching out for a short rest.

As he drove through the busy streets, Ted wondered about his passenger. His thoughts though had nothing to do with the reported shooting of the diplomat. Rather, he wondered if Michele knew about his passenger's rendezvous with another woman. It didn't matter, of course, but Ted often imagined about the lives of his fares. It made the job more interesting.

When the cab approached the hotel, the traffic came to a standstill.

"Idiots!" Ted exclaimed.

"What is it?"

"Students protesting the president's visit. You may have to get out here, the road is blocked," Ted said. "The hotel is right there." He pointed at the building a block away.

"This is fine. Thanks again, Ted." As before, Clint gave him a large tip. "We may see you later."

Once out of the taxi, Clint immediately saw a number of policemen walking alongside and keeping an eye on the marching students. A crowd had formed on the sidewalks with a few of the crowd yelling things at the marchers. Clint stayed close to the edge of the buildings and walked as quickly as he thought any foreigner would when caught near a situation like this. He entered the hotel and went straight to the elevators.

Two men watched Clint enter the hotel. The first, a policeman, called in that he saw a man who matched the description of the man involved in the shootout that morning. When asked what he was doing, the policeman said he was on duty monitoring the student protest march. He was told to stay with the protestors and someone else would check out the hotel.

At police headquarters, the police sergeant hung up his phone and turned to his immediate subordinate, "Make a note that another tall, dark haired, Caucasian foreigner was sighted. This one was seen going into the Hotel Dal. What does that make? Thirty-seven since the attack on Davenport?"

"Thirty-eight. It's getting out of hand. I think that's the second in that hotel, too."

"Could be the same guy."

"Any of them could be duplicates."

"I've already told the captain that we should focus on the train station, seaports and airports. We can do that all over the country. Let him come to us," the sergeant said.

"Think they'll listen?"

"I don't know, but after we stopped and interviewed seven of those men this morning, the Captain put a hold on our interviewing any more until we develop some additional information."

"Makes sense. Sergeant, were those guys who attacked the diplomat really from the north, like the dead guys found near Pyongtek?"

"That's the story."

"I don't remember this ever happening before. What do you think is going on?"

"Must have something to do with the American President's visit. I haven't seen anything official that says that, but I know that's the thinking at the top."

"Perhaps we should let them kill each other."

The sergeant stared at his subordinate. "Keep those thoughts to yourself. Most might agree with you, but it doesn't matter, we can't allow it on our soil. Any collateral damage, like the driver this morning, will be our people, and that we cannot permit."

"What have the Americans said about this?"

"I have no idea, but I don't believe they have taken responsibility for anything."

"That will not help their position."

"No, it won't."

CHAPTER 17

The second person to watch Clint enter the hotel was Yi Sung Minh. The leader of the North Korean assassination team had not seen Clint before, but he had no doubt this tall American was the man who had done so much damage to his team. Yi had even started to think the woman in the woods that night was not alone. This man must have been with her. He never did believe that a woman could have accomplished all that she had alone that night.

When word came to Yi that the attempt to capture the American had failed, he and his number two, Kim Moon Jin, had begun plotting a new strategy to accomplish the assassination without the information they had expected from the American, Whatley. The information would have given them an advantage, or at least Whatley had claimed it would. Yi didn't know who paid Whatley or how much he had been paid, but he had a suspicion of all Americans and their greed. It certainly wouldn't have been the first time an American had offered to sell supposedly good information to only have that information turn out to be worth a lot less than expected.

Yi did know, though, that his superiors had placed significant importance to the information. For that reason alone, he would continue pursuing this man and the woman, but the goal of the mission would stay his primary focus.

By chance, a North Korean contact working within the South Korean government had arrived in Busan from Seoul to assist the local Busan officials with the handling of the event. Like most of the North Korean sympathizers living in the south, this contact had been recruited while in college. The man worked in protocol with little access to classified information and had therefore avoided any in-depth screening by South Korean security. However, he did have access to the dignitaries planned activities and the time table of events. Yi had already made contact with the individual, and Kim should be meeting him about now.

Unlike the other North Korean assets Yi had dealt with on this mission, this one working protocol seemed motivated and could be the key to the success of their mission. He promised to provide Kim a copy of the American leader's agenda including travel routes and times.   Yi and Kim agreed that access to information like that would be as valuable as anything Whatley could have provided them.

Yi had pulled everyone off the surveillance of the hotel. He instructed them to get a good meal and some rest, while he maintained a watch of the entrance. His purpose for being here was personal. Yi wanted revenge. These two Americans had come close to wrecking his mission and had killed a number of his team. Of course, if the information that Whatley supposedly had could still be retrieved, then that would be good, too, but he doubted that the information still had any value. It seemed improbable that these two Americans hadn't shared it with Washington D.C.

Yi had telephoned Sergeant Lee Lim Kwan, the policeman he had used to get the woman's room number. Yi wanted to know what the police knew about the American man. Lee said that the police had a nationwide alert for the American and that investigators had already been sent out to a number of the hotels in Busan that foreigners frequented. Lee insisted that he was too busy to get away, but said he would call Yi if any information came to his attention about the American.

The chaos on the street with the marchers and the police watching them prevented Yi from doing something unwise. He had entertained the idea of pursuing the American into the hotel, despite knowing such a move would be rash and would put the entire operation at risk. Still, he thought, slicing the man's throat would be so satisfying.

Yi's phone rang. He walked away from the crowd on the sidewalk and answered his phone.

"Looks like our fortunes have changed," Kim Moon Jin said.

"You met with him?"

"Yes, he gave us some very interesting material. I can't believe our other source would have been this good."

"Too good to be true?" Yi asked.

"No, I think this is the real thing. I want to check out a few locations. I think by the time I meet back with you, I'll have good game plan for you."

"Good, do what you have to do. What did he want from us?"

"Very little. I'll tell you when I return."

Yi didn't like waiting for information, but he had respect for Kim and would wait for their meeting. He started thinking that it wouldn't be that bad to go after the American man and woman at some later date. What was that old North Korean saying? Revenge is sweetest served cold. Well, something like that.

He finished his coffee and walked down the block for a refill. He didn't expect the two Americans to walk out together and fall into his hands, but stranger things have happened. He stayed in the coffee shop. The angle to the hotel was bad, but he could make out the front if he leaned close to the window. Besides, Kim would be here in a few minutes and he was looking forward to finding out what pleased Kim so much.

The wait was short. His number two entered and made a beeline toward him. He carried an envelope in his left hand.

"May I get a coffee first?" he asked.

"Of course," Yi said.

"We have what we need to do the job," Kim said after he returned with a coffee in hand.

"What is it?"

"When the target is here in Busan, he plans to visit the American consulate. While there, he will be speaking to a small group of people in an outdoor setting, a small garden, a patio, or something like that. It's a very short meeting to thank everyone at the consulate for their support. From street level no one outside the grounds can see in, but there are a number of tall buildings in the area. The closest ones in will undoubtedly have a security presence, probably both American and Korean together, but the ones farther out may not have any security or only a light presence. Our contact said there are three or four very tall buildings that might provide us with a good line of sight."

"How far?" Yi asked.

"I don't know, but if I can see him, I can hit him," Kim said. "I understand you are better than me. We have two rifles."

Yi smiled. He knew Kim was flattering him with the comment. Kim's reputation as a sniper, like the rest of his reputation, was legendary. However, his point was well taken. Yi, too, was a master marksman. There was a reason they had brought with them two NSG-85 sniper rifles.

"We would have to synchronize the time of fire, but that would be easy," Yi said.

"We might not know who missed or hit the target," Kim said grinning.

"Of course, I would take credit," Yi said grinning. "No. We would report it as it happened, and we both get credit." He paused for a minute. "We will have to get back home to reap the rewards of our success."

"I have a few ideas about that," Kim said. The two huddled and finalized the first draft of their plan. They each knew it would be modified as time went by.

They agreed that the first step would be to identify which buildings they would use and what spots in each building would offer them the best location to take the shot at the president. This they would do immediately, because they had no doubts that these buildings would be closed and guarded hours before the arrival of the American leader.

Yi and Kim divided the members of what was left of their team between them. Each would be responsible for devising their team's final plan to gain access to their respective buildings. They discussed the value of creating a diversion elsewhere in the city. Yi knew that the Americans and South Koreans were already at a high state of security for the visit.

"A diversion might have more value to us after the assassination. It may help our escape from the city," Yi said.

"True," Kim said, "but it wouldn't hurt if we can get the students rioting during the visit. Our sympathizers are already working toward that goal."

"Yes. A few scattered fires in the city will also help."

"The American puppet will also be in the city tomorrow," Kim said referring to the South Korean leader. "I assume our lack of interest in him is intentional?"

"Yes, we want to embarrass him. His support among the people is low, and it is better to show him as being inept than to make him a martyr."

Kim grinned, he could already envision seeing the American leader through the scope on the rifle.

CHAPTER 18

"They've flooded customs and security checkpoints at the airports and harbors with Clint's description. He won't be able to get through," Dolly said.

Buzz nodded. He had seen the same message traffic referring to the steps the South Korean government was taking to catch Clint. "Let's get word to them to stay put. Tell them why. We'll have to figure another way."

"Should you contact Mr. Thomas?"

"Not yet. Deer may have some ideas."

"At least they still haven't put out a public bulletin requesting help in locating Clint. I bet they'll do so as soon as the state visit is over. We need to get them out of there," Dolly said.

"I'll send a text right now to Deer, see what she thinks."

"Ask her how she's doing, too."

"Of course," Buzz said, but he knew without Dolly's remark, he might not have. Deer would downplay her injury, and he would have to imagine how bad it was.

Halfway across the world the sound of her phone brought Deer out of a fitful sleep. She had sweated through her shirt. They may say that men sweat and women perspire, but she had sweated. Her head throbbed, and she needed a drink of water.

At first, she thought Clint had sent her another text. She saw it was her office and opened it. "Flight today needs to be cancelled. Clint's description distributed to all security checkpoints. Description not perfect, but good enough. Once they grab him, you will be scrutinized. May be hard to explain your injuries. Working hard to find solution. Any suggestions?"

For some reason, not leaving today was a relief. Deer didn't feel like she could handle going anywhere. She reread the text and almost laughed when she got to the word scrutinized. Only Buzz would use that word. She might have used it, too, if its root word was "screwed."

She sent a return text. "Cancel flight but do nothing else except monitor the situation here. We'll come up with plan and let you know." Deer didn't elaborate because she had no idea how they would get out of Korea and at the moment, didn't care. She forced herself out of bed and went into the bathroom, resisting the temptation to send a text to Clint asking him where he was.

A moment later, Clint entered the hotel suite and heard the water running in the bathroom. He secured all the locks and latches on the door and shoved the couch against it. He didn't expect anyone, but he didn't want to take any chances. He opened the bag on the small counter and took the medicine out of it. When Deer walked out of the bathroom, she looked like she had aged twenty years. Clint had to force himself not to say anything about her appearance.

"Think I look bad now, you should have seen me before I prettied myself up in there," she said, seeing the look in Clint's eyes.

"I got you some stuff." He motioned with his hand toward the items on the small kitchenette counter.

"Good. How did you decide what to get?"

"Had some help from a pharmacist. This antibiotic is supposed to be a good one, whatever that really means. Also, I didn't ask you if you were allergic to anything."

"Just bullets."

"The instruction sheet is inside the box. It's in English as well as about four other languages. How does it look?" Clint pointed his eyes at the bandage on her arm.

"Lousy," Deer said. She swallowed two Tylenol before looking at the instruction sheet she pulled out of the small medicine box. She wondered if with the amount of Tylenol she had taken in the last couple of days whether a Tylenol overdose now posed more of a health threat than the bullet wounds.

"Our reservations have been cancelled," she said without looking up.

"That's not good. Is it because of me?"

"Yes. What exactly happened? Did you give Davenport the info we got from Whatley?"

"We? I wasn't much help to you. My guess is that I was still in Hawaii when you were taking care of business."

Deer studied the medicine bottle and didn't say anything.

"Yes, I gave Davenport the material, and I think the attack on us made him realize its importance. He was shot, but his injury was minor. His driver died at the scene."

"How'd it happen?" Deer asked.

Clint summarized the attack and his departure from the scene.

"This woman you had lunch with, what's her involvement with you?"

"Met her at the airport. She gave me a card to her parent's restaurant and put her name and phone number on the back. I had a cab take me there after I ditched the car. I thought keeping a low profile for an hour or so couldn't hurt."

Deer nodded. "She's probably not someone we should trust to get us out of here."

"No, but if we're looking for an alternative way to get out of Korea, I may have an idea," Clint said thinking of his brief conversation with Eleanor Rivers.

"What have you got?"

"A long shot, but I think it's worth exploring. I met a woman at the park dedication this morning." He went on to identify Rivers and that he believed she was wealthy and well connected.

A few minutes later Deer sent a long text to Buzz while Clint changed clothes. She didn't expect an answer for a while. Returning her attention to the antibiotics, she decided to increase her first dose from two to three tablets and then go back down to the prescribed two tablets at a time. She needed to kick start the treatment of the infection that now had her worried. Rummaging through her backpack, she found her last power bar. Although she felt more exhausted than hungry, she forced herself to eat it.

Clint studied the clothes he had brought along and realized that there was little to offer in the selection that would do much to change his appearance. The longer he stayed in Korea the higher the odds that he would be spotted and detained by the local authorities. Once that happened, he had little doubt things would go badly. If they decided to approach Eleanor Rivers for help, he wondered how far she could be trusted. They could be digging themselves into a deeper hole.

He went back into the living room. Deer looked up at him from the couch that was pushed against the door.

"I sent a text to Buzz. We should hear back shortly. Let's hope your lady friend is clean."

"If she is, should I press ahead with going to her party tonight? While she might be able to help us, it would be better to approach her in private."

"Private is always better. It gives you the opportunity to utilize a wider variety of options to garner her support. I have found that trust and love of one's country is not always enough."

Deer's phone rang and after looking at the screen she answered it. "Hello, Buzz, sorry about the mess I created."

In the bowels or an otherwise vacant building in D.C., Buzz studied a computer screen while he talked to his boss. "Well, you know that you and I are too old to be in the field these days."

"Watch it, buster," Deer replied, making Buzz grin.

"Eleanor Rivers has no criminal past. There's nothing negative anywhere on her. The IRS has had her on their screen a couple times because she's worth several hundred million and lives outside the U.S. That naturally makes them suspicious that she's hiding income, but nothing in their files indicates she's done anything wrong. On a different topic, the Secret Service is going bananas over the note Clint gave to Davenport. They are pushing to cancel the whole visit to South Korea, but that's not going to happen. They have adjusted the itinerary to negate the possibility the North Koreans had already received the same information Clint gave Davenport."

"I don't think the North Koreans have called off the assassination attempt," Deer said.

"Me neither. The wires throughout the South are filled with speculation. There's even some war talk in their Defense Ministry."

"We don't need that."

"It shouldn't come to that, but if they succeed in assassinating the president, all bets are off. Saving face is still very important throughout Asia."

"Were you able to learn if Rivers has her own boat or plane?"

"No, but you know with that kind of money there are plenty of charter companies that are available at the snap of a finger."

"Or a wave of a credit card," Deer said.

"That's right. The company that employed her husband has a small fleet of private planes all over the world. They may have one permanently assigned to Busan. For that matter they may have access to someone's yacht."

"That's our hope. Clint is going to try to charm her tonight into helping us."

"By the way, a couple things have fallen our way."

"Like what?"

"The South Koreans, and for the most part our side of the pond, are now linking the dead guys found near Pyongtek to the three who attacked Clint earlier today. Everyone is now speculating that Clint is also responsible for the deaths of all of them."

"If push comes to shove, we can prove he wasn't in country

for the first deaths," Deer said. "That will help with those who insist on linking the two events. Are there any indications they are looking for me?"

"Nothing yet. How are you doing?"

"Not good, but Clint picked up some antibiotics that I hope will keep the infection at bay."

"We need to get both of you out of there."

"I know, and we still need to shoot for Guam, so don't try to change destinations."

"It sounds like you'll be making your own travel plans anyway. Anything we try to charter will have to go through all the usual customs and security procedures, and we may not be able to get anything in until after the big event there is over."

"That's why we're focusing on Rivers right now," Deer said.

"Ok, good luck and stay in touch."

"Hey, before you go. What's the speculation over there on what's going on?"

Buzz knew she was talking about the U.S. Intelligence Community's assessment on who was responsible for the deaths of the North Koreans.

"A lot of agencies are speculating it's a CIA or military operation in support of the state visit. Of course, everyone is denying any involvement which is spinning the curiosity up higher. Right now, figuring that out is not a priority, but it may become one later. The real priority is figuring out what the crazy guy up north is up to. Ever since he had his own half-brother assassinated with the outlawed chemical weapon and has set off a few nuclear explosions, the rest of the world has become more concerned than usual about him."

"Well, obviously he's trying to kill our president," Deer said.

"Everyone knows that by now, but any attempt is just going to turn more people against him, if that's even possible. If he wants to provoke a war he cannot win, this would be a good step in that direction."

"The guy's insane."

"Amen."

They ended the call.

"You're on, Clint. They didn't find anything bad on Rivers. You may have to charm her. Need any advice?" she grinned and Clint thought this was the first time since he arrived in Korea that she had a little spark in her eyes.

"What worked for you?"

"A little cleavage and sufficient alcohol, or maybe it was the other way around. It's been a long time."

"I may have to go about it a little differently," Clint said. He wanted to say that when she wasn't looking half dead, that she could easily still seduce about any man she wanted. However, for a variety of reasons, he didn't say anything.

CHAPTER 19

Ms. Eleanor Rivers hadn't reached her home when her phone rang. She almost didn't answer it as she was half asleep. Heavy traffic had slowed the drive, and despite her chauffeur's best efforts to find an alternate route, the car crept along with traffic that seemed to ooze, stop, and then ooze along again.

The call was from Martha Stewart. Not the famous one, but the Martha Stewart who worked for Johnny Davenport. Rivers had worked on a lot of projects in the past with Davenport, and at the ceremony, she had seen and talked to Stewart. Her first thought was that she must have left something at the ceremony.

"Hello," she said and then listened in silence while Stewart told her about the attempt on Davenport's life. "My God," she interjected more than once as she listened.

"You say Johnny's okay?"

"He was shot, but they're telling me it's not serious. His poor driver died at the scene."

"How horrible. You say someone saved his life?" Eleanor's mind raced ahead of her question. She had watched the man she talked to at the ceremony get into Davenport's car and ride away with Johnny and the driver.

"Yes, and you must not tell anyone else this. They were giving a man a ride to the consulate, and when the shooting started, this man shot and killed all three men who were trying to kill Johnny, I mean Mr. Davenport. The man then jumped into the other car and drove off."

"That sounds crazy. Who was this man?"

"No one knows. He saved Mr. Davenport, but then he fled like he was guilty of something," Stewart said.

"Where's Johnny now?"

"At the hospital. Everyone is spooked around here right now. You know, with the visit and now this. I hope they don't make Mr. Davenport work the rest of the day."

Rivers got the name of the hospital before ending the call. Thirty minutes later, she entered the hospital and found Davenport sitting alone in a private room on the third floor. He had a hospital gown wrapped around him. He was still in his slacks and shoes, but it looked he wasn't wearing anything above the waist.

"Have they not seen you yet?" Rivers asked.

"Why hello, Eleanor. I hope you didn't come here just to visit me. I'm fine."

"I heard you were shot."

"Yes, a slight graze. They've already stitched me up. I have to stay here a little longer until the drugs wear off and my ride comes to get me. I guess I'm still a little doped up."

"I thought someone would be here with you."

"There was. You missed him by a couple of minutes. One of the security guys was here getting my statement. Not much to say, you know, it all happened so fast."

"I can't believe someone was trying to assassinate you."

"Between you and me," Davenport leaned a little toward Rivers who had positioned herself in the chair next to him, "I think they may have been after the other guy."

"Other guy?"

"Yes, a big guy at the ceremony this morning wanted to talk to me. I'd never seen him before. We gave him a lift, but we hadn't gone far when this white car runs us off the road and starts shooting at us. They killed my driver; did you hear about that? It was horrible."

"Yes, that was terrible."

"This guy, the one we're giving a ride, yells at me to get down. I did, and that may have saved my life. Meanwhile, he jumps out of the car and starts shooting back at our attackers.

Then just like that it's all over, and he's gone. I only learned afterwards that three men attacked us. Three of them and this guy puts all three of them down in the blink of an eye. Can you believe that?"

"God, it's like a spy thriller. What did you tell the security officer about him?"

"Very little. He must be CIA or someone else in deep cover. I think it might be best not to say too much about him. So, this is our little secret. Okay?" He leaned a little closer to her.

"Absolutely."

"You know, Eleanor, if I wasn't married--"

"Shh! Don't go there. You are married, and it's just the drugs making you say that. I'm too old for you."

"No way," Davenport said with a big grin.

"Oh, I didn't know you had a visitor."

"Your patient seems to be doing very well," Rivers said to the tall brown-haired nurse who had entered the room and spoke perfect English.

"He had a nasty wound, and he will have the scar to show off to his grandkids, but it wasn't deep and didn't hit bone. He should be fine. Mr. Davenport, how are you feeling, a little light headed or dizzy still?"

"I feel fine. Do you know when I can go?"

"It won't be long. Your wife will be coming for you rather than someone from the consulate. You'll be going home. She should be here in about a half hour." She maneuvered closer to him. "Now let me check your bandage."

"I better be leaving, Johnny. I'll give you a call in a few days to make sure you're doing better." Rivers stood but delayed walking out until the nurse exposed the large bandage covering Davenport's right shoulder.

"Thanks for coming by," Davenport said as Rivers walked out of the room. He knew he had talked too much about the man, but he was proud of himself for not mentioning the small paper tablet that the man had given to him. He could still keep some secrets.

Rivers phone rang again while she was walking out of the hospital. This call came from the personal assistant to the Chief of Police for the city of Busan, who said his boss would not be able to make the dinner party. The call pushed Rivers to a decision she had been considering since she heard about the attempt on Davenport. She called her own personal assistant and instructed her to call the other invitees and let them know that the dinner party was cancelled due to all the things happening in the city. She would reschedule it later.

As her assistant did not have any knowledge of the man she had met that morning at the ceremony, she would not call him. He would be the only person thinking the party was still happening. Rivers knew he would most likely never contact her again, but she hoped he might. She invited him out of some pretty basic instincts and had even felt a little self-conscious after he walked away from her. She hoped she hadn't looked like a silly school girl hitting on the star quarterback.

After getting into her car, Rivers called her friend, Kwan Su Jin.

"Sue, how are you today? This is Eleanor," Rivers said. On today's smart phones one knew who was calling before they answered, but Rivers still thought it was polite to identify herself. Kwan Su Jin had attended Yale, married an American, and during her stay in the U.S. had started telling everyone to call her Sue. For twelve years in New York City she was Sue Morris. When the divorce came, she left New York and returned to her hometown of Busan. To the locals she once again became Kwan Su Jin, but to most of the international community she was Sue Kwan.

Sue never remarried and like Rivers had no interest in making that commitment again. She and Rivers had become good friends shortly after Rivers arrival in Korea. Although not nearly as wealthy as Rivers, a mutual friend had said Kwan Su Jin's wealth to be around ten million dollars.

"My dear Eleanor, what's going on in your life today?"

"Did you hear about the assassination attempt on Johnny Davenport?"

"What? When?"

"This morning, he's going to be ok. I was hoping you could tell me what's going on."

"Let me make some calls. I've been in my Yoga class this morning."

"Let me know what you hear, and I'll do the same. We could meet for drinks later."

"Not today, but I'll take a rain check," Sue said. "I'll call you later."

Rivers looked forward to hearing from Sue. The woman had ears everywhere. Although she never would admit to it, rumors had it that Sue was either working for the CIA or the South Korean equivalent.

Rivers wished she had some way to contact the man. She wondered why. She didn't know him and had no reason to think he would ever want to see her again. Maybe it wasn't the man but the mystery or the intrigue that had captured her interest. Whatever it was, she would keep her knowledge of him to herself. He had saved Johnny's life, and Johnny was a good man with a sweet family. For that deed alone, he deserved her discretion. She had no doubt that the local police would not take it lightly that he was involved in a gunfight on its turf.

On the way to her house, she asked her driver to contact some of his friends and try to find out who tried to kill Davenport. She wondered who else she could contact. Off the top of her head she couldn't think of another person whom she would feel comfortable asking. She would have to wait.

Her wait didn't last long. Shortly after she arrived home, Sue called her back.

"Guess what?" Sue asked.

"Oh, Sue, I have no idea."

"The word among the police is that the three men who attacked Davenport were North Koreans."

"North Koreans?"

"Yes, can you believe it? The city has gone into high alert."

"Do they suspect an invasion?"

"Oh, don't be silly. There's not going to be an invasion. At least I hope not. They're linking the North Koreans here with something that happened up by Seoul."

"What happened there?" Rivers asked.

"I'm not sure, but it sounds like more dead North Koreans were discovered just outside Pyongtek."

"How did they all get here?"

"Who knows, but like I said, everyone's at high alert."

"Do you think it's connected to the president's visit?"

"No one is saying that, but I think it's what they're thinking. Seems the obvious answer. Did Johnny tell you what happened?"

"Only that they were driving back to the consulate after the ceremony and were suddenly driven off the road. Three men started shooting at them."

"Who was it that shot the North Koreans?"

Rivers' antenna went up. While it was a logical question, she wondered if this was why Sue called her back so quickly.

"A man he met at the ceremony this morning. He didn't know him. A bit strange, but giving the man a ride turned out saving his life. Johnny said he has no idea why the men attacked him, and I can't believe the North Koreans would have any interest in him. I also think it must have something to do with the big visit tomorrow. Maybe they want the president to cancel the visit and embarrass South Korea."

"Is that what Johnny said?"

"Oh no, that's my own theory."

"The man had to be with the U.S. Secret Service," Sue said. "No other Americans carry weapons in our country, but why did he flee the scene?"

"I don't know unless there is more to all this than we know. It could be a joint Korean and U.S. secret operation sweeping up North Korean agents in the south before the president's arrival."

"You may have something there."

They ended the call after promising to get back together if either discovered anything new. Rivers and Sue had dozens of similar conversations in the past. Frequently, they were trying to discern what caused a divorce or why someone got fired. Once they tried to understand why an acquaintance committed suicide. This was the first time, however, where Rivers could remember that she knew a significant piece of the puzzle and had no plans to share it with Sue. She felt a little guilty, and if she never heard from Maxwell Steel again, she probably would tell Sue. Until then, though, she would keep her knowledge of the man secret.

She doubted that she would hear from Steel and spent the next few hours working in her sewing room embroidering roosters on a set of twelve linen napkins. She had started embroidering shortly after her husband's death, and what had started as a way to keep her from falling into a depression had evolved into a passion. She spent a couple hours every day in this room creating things to give away to others. It kept her mind busy, but today she noticed on more than one occasion her eyes returning to the screen of her phone as it sat quietly on a table next to her.

When her phone rang in the middle of the afternoon, she almost jumped out of her chair.

CHAPTER 20

"This is crazy," Kim Moon Jin said to Li Chang as the two of them attempted to drive through the streets of Busan.

The security measures being made for the impending state visit had already resulted in a few main road closures. In addition, the city police had set up a series of roadblocks in their search for the missing vehicle used by the now dead men who attacked the U.S. diplomat Johnny Davenport. These two separate factors caused the crazy rush hour traffic in the busy city to become unbearable.

What Kim thought would be a ten-minute drive to the tall building he would be using took forty minutes. He made a mental note to leave a lot earlier tomorrow to get here. The building did not have the modern appearance of a lot of the new construction in the city, but it would work just fine.

"Now, let's see how hard it is to get inside," Kim said.

"Not too hard," Li said and indicated to the people entering and leaving through the main entrance.

"Don't be stupid," Kim snarled.

The two walked to the front entrance and stepped inside. The large foyer had a security guard seated at a small desk near the hallway that led deeper into the building. Kim could see people in the hall lined up for what he believed to be the elevators.

"Look here," Li said.

Kim read the sign that Li had been reading. "The entire building will be closed tomorrow. That's what we thought."

A separate sign provided a list of offices in the building and their locations. "Fifteenth floor, the offices of the Sun Law Office. That's where we'll go."

Kim saw that the guard paid little attention to a couple that entered the hall. He followed the couple leaving Li still reading the sign. The guard didn't try to stop him. Kim didn't look back at Li. He had already formed the opinion that Li was one of the team's weak links, and he didn't like weak links. He also thought he noticed something in Li's behavior that had him worried. Kim couldn't put his finger on it, but after the mission, he would suggest to Yi that Li be reassigned to some desolate, internal North Korean security checkpoint for the rest of his career.

Li glanced up and saw Kim walk past the guard. He hurried behind him. In the elevator, the two were alone after the eleventh floor.

"How do you want to handle this?" Li asked.

"Not sure, just stay close and keep your eyes open. Only a couple of offices on this floor have balconies and we need to locate them."

"The Sun Law Office?"

"I don't know. That was what we were going to tell the guard if he asked where we were going."

The door opened and they walked out into a wide hallway lined with solid walls and several closed doors.

"This is going to make it harder. I was hoping we could see into the offices," Kim said and stood still thinking about the easiest way to gain access to the offices without attracting too much attention.

"I think we'll need something on this side of the building," Li said indicating the offices along the hall on his right side.

Kim nodded. "Get your phone out and pretend that you are making notes as I talk to the people in these offices."

Li wanted to ask what he was going to talk about, but he knew that Kim didn't like to be second guessed. He also felt like Kim had become impatient with him. He didn't care for Kim's superior attitude, but that was something he would most certainly keep to himself.

Kim walked up to the closest door and entered the office with

Li following him close behind. The large room they stepped into appeared to be a reception area and contained a number of desks lined up along the interior wall. Across from them a series of private offices filled the space to the exterior wall of the building. Kim could see this because three of the closest offices had large glass interior windows that allowed one to look through them into the offices. Two other doors led through solid walls further down that could lead to more offices or to storage rooms. Kim didn't see any evidence of exterior balconies.

"Hello," he said to the young woman occupying the desk closest to him. "Excuse me for troubling you, but have you noticed any electrical power surges in your offices in the last day or two?"

"No, I don't think so," she said. "Have there been some?"

"Some of the other occupants have complained. We're trying to determine which floors may have been affected."

"Let me ask our manager," she picked up the phone on her desk and pushed a button. She talked to someone before looking back up at Kim and shaking her head. "We haven't noticed anything," she said with her hand over the mouth piece.

"That's fine, thank you," Kim said. He and Li walked out, while the woman on the phone started talking about someone being sick again.

Once in the hall, Kim walked directly to the next office without saying anything to Li. He opened the door and walked in allowing the door to swing closed behind him. Li caught the door before it closed. As before, the room they entered served as a reception area, but this one provided no view to what a large interior door hid behind it.

"Welcome to the Sun Law Firm," the young, attractive lady said as she stood up and offered a slight bow. "How may we be of service?"

Kim's first thought surprised him. Usually, little could distract him from his mission. However, this receptionist had him thinking of why he couldn't find someone like her to work in his office. He found her very attractive, but her demeanor and voice grabbed him the most. She almost cooed while she talked, and her posture was old school, almost subservient. He hadn't realized that he had stood there silent for a few seconds until Li spoke up.

"We were wondering if your office has suffered any power outages in the last few days," Li asked.

Despite his own distraction, Kim wanted to yell at Li. The same approach wouldn't gain them access to the interior offices.

"No, we haven't," the receptionist answered.

"The office next door hasn't either," Kim said, and turning to Li, "It must just be confined to that one floor."

Li nodded like he was making a mental note of the comment.

"While we're here, I do have one other question. We've had some issues with the balcony doors letting in too much cold air in the winter and, although we don't notice it, allowing too much of our air conditioning to escape outside during the summer. Is it possible to take a quick look at a few of your balcony doors, or should we come back later?" Kim asked.

"Oh. We have two offices empty at the moment. I guess I could give you a quick look at those. Do you need to speak to someone in charge?"

"No, a quick glance at the doors will be all we need. If you don't mind, you can escort us," Kim said.

"Yes," she said, although her eyes gave away the fact that she was unsure if she should leave her desk. She walked them into the interior offices where several other women looked up in curiosity as the two men strode past.

"We can go into this office," she led them into a vacant room.

Kim opened and shut the sliding glass door that led out onto a private balcony. He stepped out onto the balcony and closed the door. He bent close to the door frame as though he was checking the seal the door made when closed from the outside.

"It looks like this one is fine. You say no one has complained about the cold air in the winter?" Kim asked.

"No."

"We won't need to trouble you anymore," Kim said. "If you'll escort us back out."

Again, the slight bow.

Once out of the law offices, Kim led Li to end of the hallway and looked out the window at the end of the corridor. "That vacant office will be a good location to set up. I could see the consulate, and if our target delivers his speech to his minions there on the patio as expected, I should have a good angle."

"Yes, sir," Li said. He hadn't seen the consulate, nor had he even looked for it. The soft, thick rug they walked on throughout the law office had him thinking again about the differences between North Korea and the outside world. The receptionist had made an impact on Li, too, but not in the same way as she had on Kim Moon Jin. Rather than wish she was in the north, she served as one more reason why he wanted to live out his life anywhere but North Korea.

"Let's go down and walk around this building. We need to determine the best way to get in early tomorrow," Kim said.

They took the elevator down and walked out past the security guard who didn't look up as they passed by.

"Typical sloppy performance, he wouldn't last a day in the job if it were up to me. I hope he's on duty tomorrow," Kim said.

CHAPTER 21

Yi Sung Minh took a different approach to gaining access to the building he would be using to assassinate the most powerful person in the world. He called Busan police Sergeant Lee Lim Kwan and told him to meet him in front of the building.

"But it is impossible for me to get away now," Lee had proclaimed.

"You fail me now, and you and your family will pay dearly. I expect you to be there in thirty minutes," Yi said and meant every word of his threat.

Lee swore to himself after the call. In truth, he had been working twelve hours straight and was going off duty in forty-five minutes. Unless he was called back in, which was always a possibility, he would be off for the day. He told his office he was going to meet with a couple of the investigative teams working the street in the ongoing effort to learn more about the attempt on the American diplomat's life earlier in the day but drove off to meet with the North Korean assassin.

Lee parked his police sedan next to the Busan Towers, a thirty-five-story condominium complex that towered over its neighboring buildings. He saw Yi standing near the entrance to the Towers.

One could find taller buildings in Busan, but they occupied a small area in the business district and were too far away to do any good for what Yi had in mind. He looked up at balconies above him and knew this building would work. He glanced down and saw Sergeant Lee approaching him.

"From now until it is done, you are under my command. Do you understand, Lee Lim Kwan? This mission has been directed by the Great Leader. You do not want me to go home saying that you were an obstacle to its success," Yi said, foregoing any greeting.

"Certainly, you must have some appreciation for how busy we are today."

"That is not my concern." He stared at Lee and saw the resolve in the police sergeant's eyes weaken. "Our plan is simple. We will talk to the management and gain access to a vacant condominium. It needs to be on the east side of the building and be as high as we can get."

Lee nodded and looked up at the balconies above him as Yi had done a few minutes earlier.

"I need you because you are going to explain to the manager that we need it for tomorrow as an observation platform. You will instruct him to tell no one of our plan and that we will be working with the American Secret Service. Do you have problems with that?"

"No sir." Actually, Lee had a lot of problems with everything about Yi, but he hadn't yet figured out a way to avoid this man.

The two men entered the building and went directly to an office on the ground floor that displayed a placard that read sales and rentals. Sergeant Lee identified himself as a police officer to the lone person in the office, a young woman doing something on her phone. She looked up and motioned with her hand for the two to wait a minute. Lee noticed her fingernails were painted different colors, and he could see she was texting someone, an activity that she could and should put on hold while she took care of customers. However, he had recently developed a theory by observing his own seventeen-year-old that these modern smart phones had some hypnotic power over the younger generation. He didn't understand it any better than how he could understand how quickly their fingers could bounce over the tiny keypad. It had to be some symbiotic relationship that rejected anyone over forty.

"Yes, may I help you," the young woman finally said.

Yi had wandered over to a wall and studied the pictures that displayed a variety of views from what he imagined were some of the higher floors in the building.

"These pictures, these were taken from this building, right?" Yi asked.

"Yes, we have some wonderful views. Would you like to see what we have available?"

Lee wondered if the fact that he identified himself as a police officer to her had completely avoided her conscious mind. He saw Yi look at him and nod.

Lee held up his police credentials for a second time. "We are with the police and would like to know if you have a vacant apartment with a view to the east. We are working with the American Secret Service and need access to the apartment for just one day, tomorrow."

"I don't know, we don't do daily rentals," she said.

Yi stepped forward. "You do not understand. We are not interested in renting anything. We do not plan to sleep in it or eat in it. We want to use it as an observation platform. It's a matter of national security. If you can't assist us in this simple matter, I will talk to your supervisor. If I have to do that, I will recommend he find someone to replace you in this job."

"You must have something vacant or with the owners out of town that we could look at today," Lee said in a patient a voice as he could muster.

The woman looked at both of them a second before deciding accommodation would be easier than further confrontation. Besides, her boss had already threatened her with firing earlier in the week simply because she came in a late a few times.

"On the east side and up high," she said and seemed to think for a few seconds. "How about the twenty third floor?"

"That would be great," Yi said.

She passed them a key. "2312, a two bedroom with a balcony."

"Can we hold onto the key until tomorrow evening?" Lee

asked.

"Yes, it's one of our vacancies. I'll make a note in the system that it's down for a few days, so no one will show it. Just bring back the key when you're done."

"Thank you," Lee said.

"Remember, our presence here must be kept secret," Yi said.

"I understand," she said. She made no effort to stand or say anything more while the two men left. She picked up her phone and saw that her boyfriend had replied to her text.

The two men found and entered the vacant apartment without any problem. Yi walked immediately to the balcony. He brought a small scope up to his right eye and studied the view. It took him only a few seconds to find and focus in on the consulate.

"Perfect," Yi said.

"So, you will not need me tomorrow."

"I want you with me in case I need you. It won't take long, and you can rush back to your precious job after it's over." Yi stared at Lee watching for any sign of resistance. He had already considered keeping Lee in his sight until the mission was over, but would rather not.

"Yes sir." Lee said with no fight left in his voice.

Once back out in front of the building, Yi specified a time to meet the following morning and the two, parted company. Yi sat in his parked car and called Kim Moon Jin.

"How did it go?"

"Everything's arranged," Kim answered. He knew they would have to overcome one hurdle, gaining access to a building closed to the public, but he didn't think it worth mentioning to Yi.

"Same here. I think everything is finally coming together." Before driving back to the rest of his team, Yi sent a cryptic text to a contact number he had been given before leaving North Korea. The text simply read, "All plans are finalized. Mission is a go." He didn't expect a reply and didn't receive one.

Chapter 22

"Eleanor, this is Maxwell, I met you at the ceremony this morning," Clint said.

His voice came in loud and clear over the phone. She recognized it as soon as she heard it. "Yes, nice to hear from you."

"I want to let you know I won't be able to make it to your party this evening."

"That's too bad, but I had to cancel the party. There was just too much going on," Rivers said. She wanted to add something about the attack on Davenport but didn't.

"Oh, that's too bad. What I was going to suggest was that we might meet for a drink before your party."

"I think that's a grand idea. I have tons of snacks and beverages here at my house and no one to share them with. Why don't you come over here? I can even whip up a meal if you're still hungry after we've gone through all appetizers."

"I don't want to be a bother to you," Clint said.

"No bother at all. Better than sitting here alone again all night."

"Okay, if you're sure. What's your address?"

"I'll send my car for you, say at five?"

Clint didn't like giving out his location, but he knew he would be vulnerable once he showed up at her house anyway. If she was working with the local authorities or the embassy, it would only be a matter of time.

"Five is fine. I'm at the Hotel Dal. I'll meet your driver out front, and by the way, I don't have any fancy clothes, so I'll be dressed fairly casual."

"Casual is fine. I'll see you in a couple of hours. Bring an appetite."

"I will," Clint said.

The call ended, and Clint turned to Deer. "She cancelled the party."

"I figured that part out. She still wants you to come over?"

"Yes."

"One of two things, you know."

Clint nodded.

"She's either setting you up, or she wants you for herself. She knows you drove away from the ceremony with Davenport, right?"

"Yes, but we knew all that before the call. It's a risk we need to take. If I'm snatched there at the house, I'll admit to being with Davenport. I'll tell them that I got the note that I gave to Davenport from a stranger and was attacked by someone after receiving the note. I defended myself, and that's how I ended up with the gun. I planned on turning myself in after Davenport and I arrived at the consulate, but the attack on us changed everything."

"It's weak, but I think we can make it work," Deer said. "But, my money is on her wanting you. You're this man of mystery who has shown up in her life. You know you may have to compromise your morality for the cause," she joked.

"Whatever it takes, except I'll have to draw the line at marriage."

"Don't worry, there's no time for that. She might not even be able to help us, but my guess is she has the connections to get us out of here. I'm working on a fallback, but right now I think she's the better of the two."

Clint didn't ask her about the fallback idea. They had committed to take a chance with Rivers, and his gut told him she would try to help. He didn't think her support had anything to do with his charm, if he even had any. Rather, he sensed in her a level of maturity and practicality that would understand and empathize with his situation. The trick would be in how to couch who he and Deer were and why they were involved in this mess. He knew the story would have to be something close to the truth, just not the whole truth.

Before the car arrived to pick Clint up, they requested an update from Buzz. He and Dolly had been monitoring the intelligence reporting coming out of Korea and the message traffic between the US embassy in Seoul and the consulate in Busan. Dolly made the call to Deer to provide the update.

"Buzz has fallen asleep in your chair. Can't fault him, he's been here for forty-eight hours. We've got very little to add to what we've already told you. The South Koreans are about as hyped as we've ever seen them. They still haven't released Clint's description to the public, but they've put a lot of pressure on their own security services to find him. If I had to guess, once the president's visit is over, Clint's description will be on every television channel."

"I imagine you're right. How about in our reporting?" Deer asked.

"Some commentary, but right now I think each of our agencies is thinking one of the others is involved in a covert op, so no one is pushing too hard to figure out which agency is behind everything," Dolly said.

"That's good for now, but you can count on the fact they all want to know. This will have a life of its own long after we're back home."

"Speaking of that, we've continued looking but there doesn't appear to be any dirt on Eleanor Rivers. Are you still planning on using her?"

"Yes. Clint will be going over there shortly to test the waters."

"Are you safe sitting there for so long?"

"Not much choice, but with a little luck we'll be out of here tomorrow," Deer said.

"You know, the air force has a secure flight line they use on the outskirts of Busan. Buzz and I might be able to arrange something."

"I'm sure you can, but it would have to wait until after the President's visit is over, and it would expose the two of us in a way I would rather not. Like we said, in a few days after the President is safe and at home, there's going to be one hell of an after-action review. Every government agency, including the military, will be tasked to dig deep and report anything they were involved in or did in this area during or around the visit. Let's hope this thing with Rivers works."

"Okay, boss. What else can we be doing for you?"

"Keep an eye on the intel that's bouncing around on the net. Anything that indicates that anyone is getting close to identifying us, we need to know immediately."

"Already doing that, and so far, we don't have anything except that one fair description of Clint. Nothing on you at all. You know, the description of Clint has his hair looking longer than normal. If he gave himself a real close cut it might help a little."

"Good idea, Dolly. We'll probably do that."

Dolly wished her luck and the two ended the call. Clint looked through the bedroom door at Deer. He had put on a different shirt and had shaved.

"Dolly suggested we cut your hair."

"My hair? Why's that?"

"The description Davenport gave of you had your hair longer than normal."

"I think he must have been trying to help me. He got a good look at my hair. I think it's normal length for most men."

"You're right, but if we cut it close, it will make you look different."

"How about we wait on what happens at River's place. If I get popped as soon as I get there, my hair won't make a bit of difference," Clint said.

"That's true. One step at a time. And, while I probably don't need to tell you this, if you do get arrested as soon as you show up, go peacefully. They're bound to have the place surrounded in case you make a run for it. We'll figure something out."

Ten minutes before the scheduled pick up time, Clint found a location far enough inside the hotel's lobby where someone watching the front of the hotel wouldn't be able to see him, but he could see the cars pulling into the space in front of the hotel. He waved the doorman over and explained he was waiting for a car and that the driver would be asking for Maxwell Steel. He gave the doormen a tip in advance for his efforts.

His wait didn't last five minutes before a small Mercedes parked in front of the hotel. The doorman hustled out to the car and then hurried back inside and signaled to Clint. He held the door open as Clint walked by perhaps hoping for another tip, but Clint went straight to the car.

"Mr. Steel?" the driver asked.

"Yes, are you from Ms. Rivers' house?"

"Yes, sir. I am Mr. Shane. We shall return to Ms. Rivers' house right away."

"Thank you." Clint wondered if he heard the name correctly. The driver was definitely a Korean national. Shane could be the Anglicized version of Jaen, Ja'en, or some other similar name that resulted from years of dealing with Americans.

The driver held the back-passenger door open for him, and Clint squeezed into the car.

"I can move the seat up a little," Mr. Shane said.

"Now that I'm in, I'm okay."

They drove away from the hotel. Clint scanned the area behind them and didn't like what he saw. A man jumped onto a motor scooter and started to follow them. Clint kept an eye on the man on the scooter, and after five minutes, he had no doubt the man was following them. When the hectic traffic created a space about a hundred yards between them, Clint leaned forward and instructed the driver to turn right onto a narrow side street. Cars and trucks lined both sides of the narrow road, and the Mercedes could barely squeeze through.

"Oh, Mr. Steel, this is no good," Mr. Shane said.

"Stop the car. Right here!"

The driver stopped the car and looked bewildered. "What are we doing?"

"Stay here, for two minutes only, I'll be back. Don't move."

"If someone comes--"

Clint didn't stick around to listen. He jumped out of the car and dashed behind the small truck next to the Mercedes.

Bewildered by Clint's actions, Mr. Shane watched a man drive up behind him on a motor scooter. He thought the man ought to be able to squeeze by the Mercedes as no other vehicle was coming or going. However, the man parked the scooter and started walking up to the driver's window. Shane prepared himself to avoid a confrontation. Despite Clint's request he stay there, he would offer to move the Mercedes and give the man more room to get by.

He opened the door and started to get out when the stranger shocked him by pointing a small handgun at him. The man continued approaching him and stopped only a few feet away.

"Where is he?" the gunman demanded.

"What?" Shane gagged a response. He instinctively looked at the front of the truck that Clint disappeared behind.

His assailant followed the driver's eyes and never noticed Clint move in from behind him.

The driver returned his attention to the gunman just as Clint struck the gunman. He saw the gunman's eyes widen for a split second and then lose their focus while his body started to collapse.

Shane took a half step backwards and watched as his passenger held the gunman under both armpits while he maneuvered the unconscious man into a slumped, sitting position, leaning him against the back of the small car parked in front of the adjacent truck.

Clint hurried back to the Mercedes. "Let's go," he instructed Shane.

The driver didn't need a second request and the car shot forward. "What happened, Mr. Steel? Who was that man? Why did he have a gun?"

"I'm not sure, Mr. Shane. When we get to Ms. Rivers house, I'll do my best to explain everything to you and her. Can you wait until then for a better explanation?"

"Yes, sir."

Actually, Shane still frightened and confused didn't know what he should do. The police needed to be notified, and this man in the back seat, did he pose a threat to Ms. Rivers? Would that man from the motorcycle have shot him? Why was he looking for his passenger? Did his boss know about the man?

They drove in silence. About a mile from his destination, Shane pulled the car over to the curb and stopped the car. He left the engine on.

Clint could see they hadn't arrived at anyone's house. He put his hand in his jacket pocket and gripped the small handgun he had taken a few minutes earlier from the North Korean. He didn't think the driver had noticed the acquisition.

Shane turned his head and looked at Clint. Clint could see he was sweating. "Sir, I must call Ms. Rivers and tell her what happened. I cannot put her in danger."

"Go ahead." Clint knew he could be lying, but this entire effort was a gamble. He couldn't fault the driver, no matter what the outcome.

Shane attached an earphone to his phone and tapped his phone a couple of times. In a few seconds he was talking excitedly into it. He stopped talking and turned his head back to Clint. "She wants to know if we are being followed now."

"No, we're alone now."

Shane turned his attention back to the phone and the

conversation went back to the local language, leaving Clint in the dark. The conversation ended abruptly, and Shane started driving again.

"We will be there in a few minutes."

Interesting, Clint thought. She wanted to know if they were still being followed. Of course, she may have asked Shane if anyone was hurt, or if they called the police or why not. On the bright side, he probably wouldn't be put through a lot of small talk before they got around to what was important, and she hadn't stopped Shane from bringing him to her house.

The scenery around the car changed from urban congested to a manicured golf course as the street dissected the golf course and led them into a residential neighborhood consisting of large houses with well-groomed yards. Shane took a side street that quickly became a cul-de-sac. He turned onto a driveway and paused as a metal gate swung open.

Clint looked around and saw that all but one of the five houses he could see had gated driveways and fences enclosing the yards. Rivers house looked nice, but it didn't look extravagant. Having a nice house and a yard did set one apart from the masses in this large city, but Clint realized he must have been expecting a mansion or something similar.

Shane stopped the car in the circular driveway and left the engine running while he got out and walked around the car to get Clint's door. Clint stepped out of the car before Shane reached him.

"Well, you must lead a very exciting life," Eleanor Rivers said from the open front door.

"It's a curse," Clint grinned. "How are you?"

"I'm fine. The better question is how are you?

"I'm okay. I think we need to talk."

"Sure, but first, would I be correct in instructing Shane to not say anything about what happened to you two on your drive out here?" Rivers asked.

"Yes."

"Shane, do you understand not to mention what happened today to anyone?"

"Yes, ma'am."

"The way you explained it, Mr. Steel may have saved your life."

"Yes, ma'am. My lips are sealed." He smiled when he spoke.

"Right," she replied with a grin of her own.

Shane returned to the car and drove it around the side of the house.

"He likes that expression, 'my lips are sealed.' It used to be our saying in the old days, I guess it still is." She smiled like she was reflecting on a cherished memory. "Please, come in Maxwell, or should I call you Max? I'd say we all need a drink."

Clint followed her into the house. While the outside could be described as pleasant non-descript, the inside exuded class. From the well-polished dark wood floors, to the custom-made furnishings, to the pictures on the walls, the place impressed him.

"You have a beautiful home, Eleanor."

"Thank you, come on in here."

He followed her into a kitchen that would have impressed even the most demanding on one of those "house hunter" shows. She took him to a small room that opened to the kitchen and to the backyard. A large window offered a view of a backyard floral garden that surrounded a water fountain shooting water up some three feet into the air.

A small round table covered with a yellow table cloth sat in the center of the room with two comfortable looking leather chairs arranged to give one a view outside.

"Please have a seat. What can I offer you to drink? I have everything."

A Korean woman with long dark hair appeared behind them. She looked at Rivers in anticipation. The woman looked in her thirties, but Clint knew he could easily be a decade off either way. He doubted she stood more than about four foot ten inches or weighed more than about ninety pounds.

"A beer?" Clint asked

"Michelob?"

"That would be fine."

Rivers spoke in Hangul to the woman. She bowed slightly and left the room.

"Beautiful, isn't she?"

"Yes, she is," Clint said.

"Last year she went through a hard time. A friend of mine knows her father. She doesn't speak much English, so I thought she might be the best choice to be here this evening."

Clint wondered what she meant and started thinking she had a better grasp on the situation than they had expected.

"A hard time?"

"Her husband beat her so bad she nearly died."

"What happened to him?"

"In jail for three years, her father and I are still trying to convince her to get a divorce. The culture is so male dominant here that they're having a hard time evolving. She thinks he just got carried away in beating her, not that he shouldn't have beaten her at all. Crazy."

The woman returned with the beer and a cocktail.

"Thank you," Clint said.

The woman bowed slightly and left the room.

"I can't even get her to stop bowing," Eleanor said.

"Nice and cold," Clint said after taking a sip.

Eleanor reached over with both hands and cupped Clint's left hand in hers. "Maxwell, I'm very happy you accepted my invitation. I cancelled the party for tonight after what I heard happened this morning. You need to know that I went over and visited Johnny at the hospital. He's an extremely nice guy and has always been one of my favorites. I know we have you to thank for his surviving the attack."

Chapter 23

Clint had little doubt she had rehearsed her opening approach to him, but she sounded sincere and her eyes never faltered from his.

"My name is Clint not Maxwell, and as you have probably surmised, the men who attacked us were after me, not Davenport or his driver. You need to know that I will answer every question that I can, but there are a few things that I must keep secret. It's for your safety as well."

She squeezed his hand gently before withdrawing her hands. She lifted her drink and said, "Cheers." They touched glasses.

"I'm not without my contacts in this city. Although I can piece together very little, the men who attacked you are, were from North Korea. In my mind, that makes them the bad guys. That part is simple. I also know that the security in this city is going insane. While I could write it off as a result of the president's visit, I think it's more than that."

"So, a man might make a big mistake if he limited your attributes to your beauty," Clint said.

"I don't know, I wouldn't complain, but let's don't get carried away."

"I went to see Davenport because I had information that I needed to get to the consulate."

"To the Secret Service."

"Yes. I knew the North Koreans would stop at nothing to prevent me from getting the message there, but I thought I had slipped them on my way to the dedication."

Eleanor couldn't remember Johnny mentioning anything about getting any information when she had seen him at the hospital, but why would he? The fact that he didn't made sense to her. She even appreciated his ability to keep that piece of information to himself.

"So, I can safely take it that you work for our government?"

"Let's say we are on the same side. I pose no threat to anyone, but I don't have diplomatic immunity. I have no one at the embassy I can turn to for help. I came to Korea without any thought or plan to get involved in anything like this."

"What brought you here?"

"A friend needed assistance to return to the United States. Physical assistance."

She studied him for a minute trying to work out if she should continue pressing him for information. She knew that he wouldn't have contacted her or come to her house if he didn't need her help. He took a big risk that she hadn't already reported him to the police.

"Does your being here put me at risk," she asked.

He instinctively wanted to say no, but held back. "I don't think so, but I can leave."

"No, no, I didn't mean that. Whatever you are, your secrets are safe with me. Many years ago, my husband and I did a few things for the consulate. Little things like assisting them to meet a contact they had in private. It was easy for us to rent a place for a week, but be gone the one day they needed to use it."

"A safe house," Clint said. "So, you're a secret agent yourself."

"I wish. My life has been rather boring since," Eleanor started to say since her husband died, but realized that would sound too full of self-pity. "Well, let's say for a couple years now my life's been uneventful."

"It shouldn't be," he said and raised his glass for another toast. "Now, tell me about you. How did you end up here?" He raised his hand and gestured to the surrounding area.

"A long boring story," she said.

"Then bore me."

They talked for a while about their younger days and how fate plays a critical role in one's life no matter how much planning one makes. In her case her husband's sudden death, and in Clint's case a seemingly straight forward trip almost kills him.

"The sad part about all this," her turn to motion to the room and house around her, "is that I go through periods of time when I'm content and others when I'm bored. I imagine it's me just getting old, I don't know."

The Korean woman surprised Clint by appearing next to them with another beer for him and a second cocktail for his hostess. He never heard her approach.

"A quiet one," he said as she left.

"I know, like a ninja," Eleanor laughed. "She must do it on purpose. I can't tell you how many times she's startled me, even when I've called her for something."

They talked some more, Eleanor had a lot of questions about how life in America had changed in the last fifteen years. Clint liked being with her and wished the circumstances that brought them together had been different. Their conversation helped both of them to feel more comfortable with the other, perhaps the goal they each had all along.

"Let me show you the house. I definitely could use a man's touch in some of the rooms."

"I doubt if my fashion sense will do much for you. This place looks fantastic."

She didn't rush the tour, and they stopped in one room to discuss the nuances of Korean home construction. It wasn't until they were in her bedroom, and she motioned for him to sit on the bed next to her that Clint caught on to the second inference in her comment about a man's touch. After he sat down, she leaned over and kissed him lightly on his lips. He pulled her closer to him, and before long they began undressing each other.

After a while the light began to fade outside the bedroom

window. They lay close together, their bodies no longer intertwined. Eleanor smiled to herself. She knew this man had come to see her needing something besides sex. Sure, she was still in good shape and believed it when others told her she looked younger than her age, but this man Max, or Clint, or whoever he was could have anyone he wanted. No, she knew he had contacted her because he needed something. Money? A place to hide? She didn't really care. She needed, or at least wanted something, too. She had gotten what she wanted, and now she would wait and see what he needed.

"Do you like Korean food, Clint?"

"Most of it."

"I think you'll like what we're having. I hope you can stay for dinner."

"I think I need to eat something after what you put me through." He kissed her.

"Good, we're having Kalbi beef. Most westerners who don't like Korean food still like Kalbi beef."

"Sounds great."

"There's a bathroom and shower in there. Make yourself at home, and I'll get the dinner going," she said and stood up grabbing a nearby robe.

"I don't want you to have to cook anything for me."

"My little ninja friend will do the cooking. I've been here for many years, but I still haven't mastered the cooking. I'll get her started. Can I get you anything else to drink?"

"Just ice water for me, thanks," he said and climbed out of bed.

She paused at the door to look at him. "Water it is." When she walked away, she wondered if a "trophy husband" might not be such a bad idea. She laughed to herself. Yes, it would be.

Clint decided to give her a few minutes alone and took a shower before getting dressed. He knew he would have to ask for her help in getting them out of the country and now wondered if he should have done so before he accepted her invitation into her bedroom. He would have to wait and see, and while he had some anxiety regarding how she would respond to his request, something in the back of his mind suggested to him that Ms. Eleanor Rivers had been a step ahead of him ever since he met her this morning. For all he knew, she was sitting in her dining room right now waiting for him to come out there and ask her for help.

CHAPTER 24

The blow to the side of his head surprised and hurt Li Chang. He started to jump to his feet before he realized what had happened.

"Stay awake!" Kim Moon Jin ordered.

Li nodded to Kim and Yi Sung Minh. The contingent of North Korean assassins had been decimated. Only six of the original group remained. They sat around the table listening to Yi go over the plan for the second time.

Somehow, Li Chang had dozed off while Yi talked. Kim's striking him angered him, but he was more embarrassed for falling asleep. He had never done that before. The plan would work, he had little doubt about that, and he admired the simplistic brilliance of it, but he didn't need to hear it again. He would be tagging along with Kim. His role required no thinking at all, follow Kim and do what he was told.

The briefing had relevance for the three team members who would be operating away from the two shooters. Their role included a series of diversionary actions. Fires, road blockages, even an explosion, but all would take place away from the presidential route. The goal would be to draw resources away from the part of the city where Kim and Yi would set up. The pattern of these incidents would have the objective of focusing South Korean security forces personnel and attention elsewhere. In reality, these diversions had less to do with the assassination and more to do with Kim and Yi making good their escape.

If things went according to plan, there would even be some fireworks going off near the consulate shortly before the president's arrival. Anything and everything to add confusion and misdirection, Sun Tzu would be proud of the plan.

"Any questions about the plan?" Yi asked.

Silence.

"Any questions about how we return home?"

Again silence.

"About anything?"

"How do you think the Americans will react to their president's assassination?" Li asked.

While they had all wondered this and a few had even broached this question among themselves in private, this was the first time anyone asked Yi this while they were all together.

"That is not your concern, and you know second guessing an assignment is never a wise thing to do," Yi said.

"Sir, I do not mean to question the wisdom of the plan or challenge anyone. I was only wondering what the Americans might do."

"The cowards will do nothing. They will weep and wring their hands, but in the end, they will do nothing. They never do anything. Their puppets here in the south will lose face, and the government may even fall. Some may even blame them for the act. Their so called free press can be so easily manipulated. Li Chang, do not say another word of this, do you understand?" Yi's eyes carried a threat that Li couldn't help but see.

Li Chang nodded and agreed. The meeting ended, and all but Kim and Yi left the room. Kim drank the last of his soju.

"I recommend when we return that you have Li Chang reassigned to a coastal village where he can rot out the rest of his years doing the least amount of harm possible."

Yi nodded. "I agree with you, brother. Should I assign someone else to you tomorrow?"

"No, he would screw up anything he was assigned to do elsewhere. Leave him with me. He only has to guard a closed door in an empty building. If he doesn't have to do it for too long, he'll manage."

"If he puts the mission in danger, you know he doesn't have

to return with us?"

"I know. Do you trust your police sergeant?"

"Only to get me into the building if there is trouble. I do not plan to let him live once I'm in place," Yi said. "He would break down one day and tell on us, and I'm afraid that might be sooner than later."

"Does he know that we will have two shooters?"

"No, I may be the best diversion of all, if they come to arrest me tomorrow."

"I will not miss," Kim said.

"I know. Even if they get me, our mission will succeed, brother."

The two men shook hands. They knew in a little more than fifteen hours, they would strike a blow that could change the world forever.

CHAPTER 25

Theresa Deer bent over the toilet. She felt nauseous and dizzy and hoped it was the side effects from the medicine Clint had gotten for her. She looked at her watch.

"Be patient, girl," she said to herself. The next twenty-four to forty-eight hours would have to bring everything to a close.

While she still believed everything would end well, the first thoughts of giving up and ending it all had started festering in her mind. Not that she would surrender to the authorities; that would be cowardly and could be very dangerous for all those who worked for her. However, sneaking off somewhere where she could hide herself and silently end it all started to have a strange attraction. She knew it was the infection affecting her mind, but the thoughts were still there.

She returned to the bedroom and considered trying to take another nap when she heard a sound at the front door. She froze and listened. She heard a click and then saw the door slowly open. Deer scrambled out of sight and searched the bedroom with her eyes looking for the pistol Clint had left behind. She remembered she had slipped it into the dresser under some items of clothing. Moving for it would make her visible to someone in the outer room.

She mentally kicked herself for not double locking the hotel room door with one of the interior latches or locks. She knew that Clint had hung the Do Not Disturb sign on the outside of the door, so whoever had entered had not come in to clean the room. Besides, hotel employees normally announce themselves when they enter a guest's room.

The intruder moved silently, but Theresa heard the sound of a zipper being slid open. Clint had left his carry on, a gym bag, next to the couch. Deer peeked around the door and saw a young man with his back to her bent over the gym bag. He wouldn't find anything in there besides dirty clothes. Knowing she only had seconds to get to the gun, Deer took three quick steps to the dresser and pulled out the drawer. She reached for the weapon and looked back at the man. He had heard her and had jumped up, turned, and now faced her.

She saw that he did not appear to be armed and noticed that he looked more afraid than she would have expected. She had her hand on the weapon but paused and left it in the drawer. The man wore a nametag and was dressed like a hotel employee. His face had a pimply, barely past adolescence appearance.

"What are you doing here?" she asked. She kept her voice firm but not loud.

"I just came to check on the mini-bar," he stammered.

"In there?" she asked, her eyes moving down to the gym bag at his feet.

His face turned white.

Deer realized this man had entered the room to steal whatever valuables he could find. He had expected the room to be vacant. "Get out and consider yourself lucky that I don't have the time to report you to the management."

The man, not a North Korean assassin but a simple thief, dashed to the door and disappeared into the hall.

Deer went to the door and used the inside latch to add the extra layer of security. She realized she was shaking. That surprised her until she decided that the shakes were likely caused by her physical condition rather than fear.

She looked at her watch. Clint had only been gone an hour. She didn't expect any message from him until late into the evening. In an effort to get her mind off herself, she sent a text to Buzz asking if he had anything new. She knew this, too, was out of character for her since she had confidence that Buzz would keep her posted on relevant news.

By chance, as she sent the text to Buzz, one appeared on her phone from her Washington D.C. office. She clicked on it and read the text.

"Interesting intelligence being developed today out of North Korea. Intercepts indicate a national celebration being planned for tomorrow afternoon. No historical precedent for celebrations for any day this week, to include tomorrow. Could mean they are expecting something to happen?"

"We all know what that means," Deer said to the empty room. On her phone she typed, "Must mean they are pressing forward w/o Whatley info."

She saw no need to ask what the Secret Service would be doing. They would be jumping through hoops and doing their best to cut the trip short. She also knew better than to ask what she could do. She and Clint were spectators now.

Back in Washington D.C., Buzz reread the text. "Who the hell is Whatley?" he said out loud. He almost asked her in a text but decided not to. She could explain later if she wanted, and he could do some discreet research on his own.

Buzz started tapping on his phone. "We agree. Everyone is already on max alert. President's visit being cut short a few hours, but is not being cancelled. No sign of a heightened security alert in the north. No strange troop movements. Whatever is going to happen will happen at your location."

"I think so, too. Could be the target has changed to South Korean leader who's less popular here than our president is back home, if that's possible," Deer responded.

"Not a good decade for heads of state anywhere."

Deer grinned. He was right. Elections across the globe had been tumultuous the last few years. Even here in Korea, the last president was booted out of office and now faced criminal charges. While Deer voted, she never considered herself political, didn't donate money to political causes, and would rather be forced to babysit than campaign for any politician. In her mind, all politicians brought their own baggage with them to the office. The old saying "Beauty is only skin deep" should be a warning sign on all politicians. She didn't know what she detested the most. The fact that most elected officials got rich in jobs that had salaries that should have kept them solidly in the middle class, or that so many were in the pockets of small groups of other people or interests.

Another text from Buzz appeared on her phone. "By the way, how are you doing?"

"Like Wiley Coyote at the end of one of those Roadrunner cartoons, but I'll make it."

"Stay tough" and a happy face appeared in the return text.

She turned the phone off and decided to try to make herself presentable in case the call from Clint came in sooner rather than later.

Back in D.C., Buzz sat his phone down on the desk and looked at Dolly. "Do you know a guy named Whatley?"

"No, although I don't always ask the men I bring home their names," Dolly grinned.

Buzz stared at the wall for a moment before looking back at Dolly. "One of the men killed near Pyongtek was believed to be an American, right?"

"Yes, a westerner for sure. What are you thinking?"

"Well, not to try to snoop on our boss, but so we can a better understand what's going on, let's suppose the American killed by Pyongtek was named Whatley – probably his last name. We already have good reason to believe Deer was in the middle of all that."

"You think she and this guy Whatley went after the North Koreans or vice-versa?" Dolly asked.

"Not sure, but with all the message traffic going on there's little doubt everyone's concerned about a threat to the president. There's also little doubt the threat is coming from North Korea."

"Obviously, so what are you getting at?"

"In her text she said," Buzz picked up his phone and studied the screen. "Let's see, she said, 'Must mean they are pressing forward without Whatley info.' So, who the hell is Whatley? The dead American?"

"And," Dolly picked up on the line of logic, "why would the little buggers be getting info from him supposedly about the president's visit?"

"That's the question."

"Damn, he was her target. She shot his ass dead and took on all those commies by herself. Damn, he was American. I didn't think we did those?"

"Have you ever seen any book of rules in this place?" Buzz asked, but he knew she was right.

"Could be why she took on this assignment by herself," Dolly said.

"Could be," Buzz nodded. "Could be why the big guy is involved," he said, referring to Leon Thomas.

"Not that knowing this does a damn thing to help get Clint and the boss out of this mess. Should we even try to find out who Whatley is or was?"

"No. Let's leave it alone. Can we get someone else into Korea in the next twenty-four hours to help get Deer out?"

"You mean leave Clint behind?"

"If necessary. He can at least hide for a while. Deer needs medical attention, and she won't go to a doctor in Korea because she'd rather die than compromise this office."

"I know," Dolly said. "We have the Black Widow on standby. She can get there in," Dolly looked at her watch, "twenty-six hours, if we give her the green light right now."

"Let's do it, and don't call her the Black Widow."

"Well she is. She's black, she's a widow, and she's very good at killing."

"Still, she might not like it," Buzz said.

"I was thinking of Stud Muffin for Clint."

Despite trying not to, Buzz couldn't help grinning. "I still can't believe you still have a security clearance."

CHAPTER 26

Clint found his hostess in the kitchen tasting a meat dish that he assumed had been prepared for dinner. Somewhere between the bedroom and the kitchen she had changed into dark blue slacks and a coral short sleeve blouse.

"It's good. Want a bite?" she asked.

"Sure."

She held a clean fork out for him. Using it, he took a small piece of meat off the serving dish.

He nodded, "Very good." A slight spicy aroma drifted in the air. It hadn't come from the meat.

The Korean woman appeared in the doorway to the dining room and said something. Eleanor Rivers smiled and replied to her.

She then turned to Clint. "Let's go eat."

"As you have probably already figured out, Eleanor, I need your help," Clint said after the two had finished the first course which consisted of a spicy soup, the source of the aroma he had noticed.

She looked at him, locking his eyes in hers. She said nothing.

"I need to get a friend, another US citizen, out of the country as soon as possible. I don't need money. I can pay for the travel, but due to the circumstances we can't simply fly out on a commercial jet. I was hoping you might have access to a private plane, a corporate jet, or even a charter."

"That's all?" she asked.

"Yes. It may not seem like much, but it really would be a life saver."

"If you have the money couldn't you simply charter the plane?"

"Yes, but we need to keep a low, a very low profile. After the incident earlier today, the Koreans have posted a likeness of me at the security checkpoints at the airports and maybe elsewhere."

"How about your friend?"

"She's been shot and refuses to see a doctor in Korea."

"Shot?" her eyes widened but only for a second. "That's silly, the doctors here are great. The hospitals, too."

Clint guessed it would take a lot to shock this lady in front of him, not that he wanted to shock her.

"It's not that. We have concerns that whoever treats her will report her to the authorities, and she has good reasons why she doesn't want that to happen."

"A she? What is she to you?"

"A co-worker, there's nothing personal between us. Never has been," Clint said. He almost added that she was a lot older but caught himself in time. He figured Rivers might be about the same age or even a year or two older than Deer.

"I still don't understand why you can't get help from the consulate. They can get you out without involving the Koreans."

"It's more complicated than that. We have passports, and you won't be violating any laws in helping us get out."

"And you want to leave tomorrow, is that right?"

"Yes, as soon as possible."

"Where do you need to go?" she asked.

"Guam, if that's possible."

"Okay. That shouldn't be hard. Just the two of you?"

"Yes."

"No weapons or any contraband?"

"No. I did leave the weapon I removed from the man who threatened your driver under the seat in the car. I didn't think you'd want me bringing it into your house."

"Oh. I wouldn't, but what's going to happen to it?"

"I can take it apart and dispose of it in different trash containers, or we could bury pieces of it. I didn't arrive in country with any weapons or expect to need one."

The main course arrived and for the moment the two stopped talking and ate. The portions on the plates were small, but a large amount of meat and vegetables remained on the platter that sat on the table between them.

"This is delicious," Clint said. "Do you mind?" He nodded at the platter.

"Please."

Clint took a second helping.

Rivers smiled but ignored his comment about the food. "I will have to go with you to Guam."

He looked up at her. "That's not necessary."

"If you want to get through Customs without drawing attention to yourselves, it is," she responded. While her statement was true, she also wanted to go with him for a variety of reasons, not the least of which was pure curiosity. She wanted to meet this woman co-worker and get a feel for her. She did not know much about Clint, but her intuition told her that she could trust him, and he needed her help. Finally, she and her husband used to take vacations in Guam. She had thoroughly enjoyed those trips but had not returned to the island since his death. Perhaps it was time.

"The man in charge of Customs at the airport is a friend of mine. With the president's visit, tomorrow will be a mad house everywhere. I think I can call him and arrange to have one of his agents meet me at the plane to take care of everything. If things haven't changed too much we won't have any problem."

"Thank you."

She smiled at him. "I need a vacation anyway. Have you been to Guam before?"

"No, never have."

She told him about her past visits there with her husband. Clint could tell she enjoyed the memories and seemed to have a genuine fondness for the island.

"After Hawaii, Guam is the honeymoon destination of choice

for Koreans. That is if they're honeymooning abroad. You'll see why when we get there. When would you want to leave?"

"Late morning, any time before noon."

When her young helper came in with coffee and dessert, Rivers asked for her phone. She pressed a series of numbers before smiling at Clint.

"Steve, this is Eleanor," she said into the phone. She listened for a moment and then made small talk for a minute before asking him if he might be able to fly her and a couple friends to Guam. "In the morning if we could, we'd like to be in the air by noon so we can get down there before too late."

She listened some more and nodded at Clint. "That would be great, Steve. We'll be there."

"The plane will be ready at 11:30," she said after getting off the phone. "I hope that's okay. He didn't think he could get away any earlier than that."

"That's perfect, and I'll pay for it all."

"If you insist. I have an account with his service, and he keeps a hefty amount of my money in escrow so he's always one or two flights ahead. Makes it easier to get his service on short notice, and he knows he won't ever get shortchanged by his clients. My husband used to use him at least once a month, and I still use him a few times a year."

"A one-man operation?"

"No, he's retired air force, ours not Korean, and he has two other former air force pilots that work for him. At least he used to. He has a jet for the longer trips and a twin-engine propeller airplane for the shorter flights. I imagine to Guam we'll get the jet."

"Thanks. How stringent are the customs or security checks on those flights?"

"Usually, they're very relaxed. I'll call my contact at customs in a minute and arrange things."

"I don't want you to do anything illegal. Like I said, we won't have any contraband. I'm worried about them detaining me because of a description they may have of me after the incident this morning," Clint said.

"Do you really think they have your description?"

"Yes, I'm fairly certain they do. I don't blame them, but I don't want to be detained. Like I said, it's rather complicated."

"You don't have to explain anymore," she said. "More coffee?"

"No, but thanks, it was good."

"So, I can handle the part at the airport, but how do you want to handle getting your friend or co-worker, as I think you said, to the airport. You said she was injured, shot, right?"

"Yes."

"It would be easier if she were to come here tonight or as early in the morning as possible. With all the activity around the president's visit traffic will be a mess. Everything will take longer."

"When would you prefer?" Clint asked.

"They're obviously watching for you, so I think it would be safer for you to stay here tonight." She put her hand over his giving Clint the impression she had a second reason why she wanted to keep him overnight. "Will her spending the night here be a problem?"

"No, not at all."

"Since they are watching for you, why don't I go get her and bring her here right now?"

"I don't want to put you in any danger."

"They don't know who I am, and we gals are masters at disguise."

"They might recognize your car."

"I have more than one car, of course," she said.

"Sorry, I'm not trying to say that you haven't thought this through, but I don't want anything to happen to you."

"Here's my plan."

CHAPTER 27

This latest loss of one more member of his team infuriated Yi Sung Minh. He had been handpicked to lead this team into South Korea, and so far, everything, well, almost everything had gone wrong. What worried Yi the most was that this member had seemingly vanished. The man left his post abruptly to follow the tall American when the American left the hotel and had never reported back. Yi hadn't heard anything on the local news channels or from his South Korean contacts that might indicate his man or the American had been killed or arrested by the police.

Yi's worst fear was that this subordinate may have defected. He tried to remember how much the man might know about the specifics of the assassination plan. He didn't know enough to pinpoint the locations where he and Kim would be setting up, but he could certainly spook the Americans into changing their itinerary and perhaps cause the American leader to leave the country early.

Things only had to hold together a few more hours, he thought. By dawn his team would be scattering to fulfill their various tasks. By noon they would all be taking their separate escape routes meeting up at the small port in Chinhae and boarding an old fishing trawler that would leave at three in the afternoon. The boat would not wait for anyone.

Yi set his alarm and tried to get some sleep. He knew he needed to be at his best in the morning.

In a nearby room, Kim Moon Jin lay in bed. He, too, lay awake, but for Kim the fact that he was not yet asleep had nothing to do with his nerves or the missing team member. Kim had cleared his mind of all outside thoughts and focused his mind on the task ahead. He visualized himself on the balcony and focusing the scope of the sniper rifle on his target. His mind ran through various possibilities, and he prepped himself for rapidly adjusting to each one so he could successfully kill the target. In his mind's eye, for the third time he clicked off all the variables he could imagine. He saw the president flinch and step back as an errant shot by Yi hit him in the shoulder. Kim would not let this surprise him or cause him to hesitate. Instead, he would instantly make the slight adjustment to his aim and make the kill shot. He envisioned his target walking among his small audience rather than standing still in front of them. This would make the shot more difficult, but he would wait until the target paused or stopped to shake someone's hand. What if the target spoke from behind a bullet proof podium? What if he went to the audience and sat in a chair among them? What if the event's timing was moved up or back?

Kim worked through each possibility and calmly planned an effective response to each. When he finally fell asleep, someone observing him would think he didn't have a care in the world. More evidence, those who knew him would say, that the man had ice running through his veins.

Across the city of Busan, Sergeant Lee Lim Kwan sat awake in his kitchen. His wife and teenage children had already gone to their rooms to get ready for bed. He knew his oldest son would remain awake for hours doing things on his iPad. The thing had cost Lee a fortune, and he hated the way it seemed to consume all of his son's time. Tonight, though, his mind was not concerned with his son.

Sergeant Lee felt like throwing up. Early tomorrow, he would be facilitating the murder of a world leader and a friend to his own country. He stared at the police issued pistol in his hand. If he was a braver man, he thought, he would've already gone somewhere where he could have killed himself in private. He would do it where his family would not have to witness the end result. He had been to crime scenes in homes of men and women who had committed suicide with knives or guns. How thoughtless could a person be to leave that vision permanently burned into the minds of one's own family?   Yet he had witnessed it over and over again, where a person so filled with self-pity or self-loathing that they never considered the horrible thing they were doing to their loved ones. No, if he had the courage, he would find some spot in a grungy alley and put a round in his head.

He wondered though, perhaps not doing so wasn't a lack of courage. Maybe he simply wanted to spend more time with his family. He had never been the best husband or father, too often giving the job a higher priority. Why had he done that? He had little doubt that if given the choice between his career or his family, he would choose family. Yet when not forced to make that choice, he had willingly given the job the vast majority of his time and attention.

He rationalized that he was only now cooperating with the North Korean assassins because of the threat to his wife and children if he didn't cooperate. How ironic it would be if in enabling the assassination of the American president, he brought about a war that resulted in thousands of deaths, perhaps even the deaths of his own family. His eyes passed back and forth between the pistol and his phone only a few steps away. What would happen to him if he made the call to his superiors? Even if he was punished, could they protect his children, his wife?

In the end, Lee did neither. He knew both options would end the relationship with his family. While he might continue to stay alive if he turned himself in, he had little doubt that he would spend the rest of his days in prison. The only way he would see his family again would be through iron bars.

CHAPTER 28

"Clint," Deer said when she answered the phone. "You okay?"

"Yes, things have been arranged. I'd like for you to come out here for the night. Traffic in the morning may be hectic."

"That's fine with me. Is Rivers fine with everything?"

"Yes. I think you'll like her. If you can cram everything I have in my suitcase, I'll call the front desk, check out, and arrange for one of the hotel staff to help you get the bags downstairs. Rivers will come get you."

"Does she know what she's getting herself into?"

"Yes. One of the men who had been following you attempted to grab or kill me on my way here. Scared the driver a bit."

"I imagine it did. Everyone okay?"

"Yes, but I had to fill in Rivers a little. She had also talked to Davenport, so she had figured some things out already?" Clint said.

"Personal curiosity or more?"

"Pretty sure it's just curiosity. How are you doing? The medicine doing any good?"

"I think so. When will she be here?"

"It's about a twenty-minute drive, so how about a half hour from now? She'll come into the lobby. She'll be in a different car than the one they used to bring me here."

"She thinks you'd be recognized and followed again?"

"Yes."

"Smart lady. We'll get along well. What does she think I am to you?"

"Just a co-worker."

"Okay. I'll be downstairs in a half hour. If anything changes, text me."

"Will do."

When the call ended, Clint looked around the room. Eleanor Rivers had gone to her room but had asked Clint to shout at her after he finished the call. He started to go find her when he almost bumped into the little ninja bringing a silver tray with a pot of coffee and cups into the room.

"You are a quiet one," he said to the young woman.

She smiled and bowed slightly before setting the tray down on a side table next to the door. "For you please," she said in heavily accented English and started to turn away.

"Thank you, please tell Ms. Rivers that I need to talk to her," Clint said.

"No need," Rivers said and entered the room, "I'm here. How did your call go?"

"She's fine with our plan and will be waiting for you in the hotel lobby. She'll have some luggage, but I'm sure someone at the hotel will help you get it into the car. Will your driver be nervous about making a second trip today to the hotel?"

"He would never admit it, if he was," Rivers said. "I've already asked him to be out front in the Hyundai. It blends in better than the Mercedes. Does your friend need a wheel chair or other assistance in getting around?"

Clint hesitated before answering. It was actually a good question; his plan at one time was to push her through the commercial airport in a wheel chair. "She should be okay for short distances."

"I have an old one in the garage. It should still work."

"We might want to use it tomorrow, but tonight she should be fine."

"Then I'll get going," she said and started to turn away. "By the way, you've never told me her name."

Clint had expected this question for some time but hoped she might not ask. "Would you mind if she told you that. I don't know what name she used when she registered at the hotel. I doubt if I know her real name."

"What a fascinating world you must live in," she leaned in and kissed Clint on the lips. When she turned and left, Clint didn't see the smile on her lips.

"Coffee?"

"Sure, why not?" Clint said. The woman had stood quietly behind him the whole time he had talked to Rivers. He had almost forgotten she was there. "How much English do you speak?"

"A little," she said. "Not very good."

"Well, I thank you for the delicious dinner tonight. Ms. Rivers is very lucky to have you help her."

The woman smiled and bowed slightly before leaving the room without saying a word. Clint watched her leave and wished he could stick around to have a man to man talk with her husband when he got out of prison.

He selected a comfortable looking chair and called the hotel. The clerk reassured him someone would be up to collect the luggage in a few minutes. He hoped that Deer would be ready.

At the hotel, Deer tossed the last of Clint's dirty clothes into his suitcase. She looked around the room before sitting down on the couch. She felt a little dizzy and nauseous.

"Get a grip, girl," she said aloud and massaged her temples. Twenty-four more hours, she had to last twenty-four more hours.

The knocking on the hotel door made her jump. She must have fallen asleep. After peering out the door's peep hole, Deer let the young man in to get their luggage. Thankfully it was not the same man who had attempted to burgle their room earlier in the day. In the elevator, he kept glancing at her. Deer thought with the way she looked, he was probably wondering if she was going to throw up on him.

In the lobby, she went straight to a vinyl couch that faced the entrance to the hotel. After she sat down, the young man set the luggage cart next to her and assumed a position near the front counter. A single receptionist, a much older man, stood behind the counter and appeared to be absorbed with something on his computer screen.

Deer brushed a drop of perspiration away from her eye and wondered if she was running a fever. A black van pulled up in front of the hotel, and four people piled out. They came in loud and laughing. Deer pegged them as American press done for the night and most likely coming from a few hours spent where alcohol flowed freely.

The three women and one man didn't give her a second glance as they walked through the lobby to the elevator. Deer hoped that tomorrow wouldn't bring them the most important story they would ever cover, the assassination of the President of the United States of America.

The headlights of another vehicle stopping in the small circular driveway of the hotel caught her attention. A lone man entered the hotel and walked up to the counter. She could hear him say something about having reservations. Another American, she thought. After a few minutes the man walked back out of the hotel and drove away.

Ten minutes later, Deer found herself fighting to stay awake. A car drove up to the hotel and the momentary flash of the headlights in her eyes chased cobwebs of fatigue away. A lone woman climbed out of the car and entered the hotel. Her eyes immediately went to Deer, and she approached her without hesitation.

In the few seconds it took Rivers to get through the hotel door and get close enough for both of them to talk without raising their voices, the two women completed their preliminary sizing up of each other.

Deer watched for any indication that something might be wrong, but she didn't see any hesitation or fear in Rivers' face, nor did she see her make any type of gesture with her hands or face that might indicate to an accomplice observing her that she had their suspect in sight. Rather what Deer saw was an attractive woman, about her own age, walking with the self-confidence of a woman who should not be underestimated.

Despite her efforts to the contrary, Rivers knew she wanted to see what Clint's co-worker looked like. She hoped the woman might be unattractive. A silly, immature attitude but Rivers couldn't fight the emotion. What she saw surprised her despite Clint's remarks. The woman on the couch looked like she had been sick for a long time. She had the appearance of someone who had given up on taking care of her looks. On the other hand, in addition to the fatigue in her eyes, Rivers could see the woman was studying her, too.

"Clint said you might need a ride," Rivers said.

"I sure do," Deer said and forced herself to stand.

"Eleanor Rivers," Rivers said and held out her hand.

"Sara Lynn," Deer said. "I appreciate your help, Eleanor."

The bellhop approached them and asked if he could help. Both women said yes, and he followed the two out to the Hyundai.

Rivers opened the back door of the car for Deer, and as Deer started to get in she gently took Deer's arm to help her. Deer flinched in pain.

They both said "sorry" in unison bringing a concerned smile to Rivers' face and a smile that looked more like a grimace to Deer's. Rivers hurried around to the other side of the car and got into the back seat next to Deer.

"Let's go home," she said to her driver.

The car pulled away from the hotel. Neither woman looked around to see if they were being followed. Although they didn't know it, no one watched the front entrance of the hotel. The leader of the North Korean assassination team had ordered everyone to bed. The tall American man and the American woman were no longer relevant; it was too late to change plans, and Yi couldn't afford to lose anyone else.

"You know, I have a good local doctor that is known for his discretion," Rivers said.

"I thank you, but if you can get us to Guam tomorrow, I already have an appointment. I'd rather hold off until then."

"Okay," Rivers said. The woman looked sick, and for a moment, Rivers wondered if her passenger was contagious. She put that thought aside remembering that Clint said the woman suffered a gunshot wound. "South Korea is normally a very pleasant place to visit and the people here are normally friendly. Sorry that your trip here hasn't….well, I guess I should just say that I hope you get to visit South Korea again sometime under better conditions."

Deer knew the woman felt like she had to say something, if only to be polite. Deer would've been happy riding all the way in silence, but she, too, knew Rivers was sticking her neck out for her and certainly didn't have to. She would return the same courtesy.

"I know. I was here years ago for a few days. It's a beautiful place. I kind of messed up this visit. Didn't get to do any touristy things at all," Deer managed a smile. "How long have you lived here?"

"A long time," Rivers said. "I keep thinking it's time for me to head back to the states, but I never get around to setting a date."

The two talked about irrelevant things for the entire ride, but by the time the car stopped in front of Rivers' home, the conversation had allowed the two women to become comfortable with each other.

CHAPTER 29

Clint heard the front door open but remained in the sun room drinking his coffee. He heard the women before he saw them and stood up when they entered the room.

"Good, the coffee is already made," Rivers said. "Why don't you sit over here, Sara." Rivers glanced at Clint when she said the name and gave him a look that said, "So, now you know what to call her."

Clint grinned back. "Any problems?"

Deer answered him first, "No, Eleanor offered coffee, and I realized how badly I needed some. By the way, Eleanor, I love what I've seen of your house."

"You seem to be doing better," Clint said.

"I'll make it," Deer said, her voice not at all convincing.

Rivers poured two cups of coffee and refilled Clint's cup. "I've explained to Clint about my pilot and the process for tomorrow. I really don't think we'll have any problem at all. There will be the usual perfunctory customs check of course, but as we won't have anything to hide, other than your face," she smiled at Clint when she said this, "we should be good."

"As I mentioned in the car," Deer said, "we certainly appreciate this."

"You've brought a little excitement into my life. It hasn't exactly had much of that these past few years. Besides from everything I can piece together, you guys are on the good side. Johnny Davenport and his wife are friends of mine, and I watch enough television to imagine you must be one, or two, of the Mission Impossible types. You know, where the message self-destructs and no one will admit to knowing you."

Her comment made Deer smile and she almost nodded.

"You're a bright woman, Eleanor. TV has a habit of glamorizing and sensationalizing real life, but we're definitely not the bad guys." She took a sip of coffee. "Oh, this is delicious."

"How about some of the left-over dessert?"

"No, I don't want you to go to any trouble," Deer said and realized how ludicrous she must sound after all the trouble they've already brought into Rivers' life.

For her part, Rivers only smiled and left the room.

"I guess that was a dumb comment," Deer said to Clint. "You doing alright?"

"I'm doing fine. Seriously, how are you?"

"I feel like crap, but I will make it." She emphasized the word "will."

"Here we go," Rivers said, returning with a large tray of desserts. "I've sent my little ninja friend home," she said to Clint.

"Do you refer to her as a house keeper or a cook? What is the proper term these days?" Clint asked.

"I call her by her name and refer to her as my friend. I pay her a salary, but it's all informal. She may or may not report it to the Korean tax authorities. I don't. Now Clint, I want you to try these," Rivers put two small plates on the coffee table next to him. One contained a piece of pie and one had what looked like a round pastry with a peach or apricot compote dabbed on top.

"Looks great," he said.

She displayed the tray in front of Deer. "Can I entice you into one of these?"

Deer didn't feel like eating but took the smallest of the pastries.

Rivers and Deer talked about some of the furniture in the room and the house while the three drank their coffee and ate the desserts. When Rivers stood to gather the plates, she turned to Clint. "Do you need any help making any reservations or getting around once we're in Guam?"

"No, but once I get Sara to the doctor, my work is done. I

could sure use someone to show me around the island," he grinned, and she smiled back.

"I'd be happy to do that, but you can't simply drop Sara off and then ignore her."

Deer almost choked on her last sip of coffee and sputtered out a laugh. "Oh, that hurt. Believe me, Eleanor, while I appreciate Clint coming here on short notice to help me make the trip back, I have zero expectation for Clint to hang around me or Guam while I recuperate. In fact, I plan on telling the doctor to give me something to let me sleep for at least a full day after he or she is done with me."

"See," Clint said to Rivers, "she wants to be ignored."

They talked for a few more minutes before Deer mentioned that she wanted to clean up and get some sleep. Rivers led her out of the room. Clint sipped on the coffee and when Rivers didn't return right away, he glanced at his phone. Nothing. He didn't have a chance to talk to Deer about anything she may have heard from D.C., so he sent a text to Buzz.

"Everything's a go for tomorrow. Should be leaving by noon. Anything we should know?"

A return text displayed on his screen a few moments later. "Glad to hear that. Still a lot of msg traffic speculating what's going on and heightened concerns about NK, but nothing specific."

"Hope you two haven't been sleeping at the office."

"Once you two get to Guam, the two of us are out of here, but until then we're going to stay on top of this. BTW, the note you passed onto Davenport has caused quite a stir within the Secret Service. They changed part of the president's itinerary today and have started an internal inquiry to determine how the route info got compromised."

"How so?" Clint asked in his return text.

"Not sure but the info described a spot and time on the route where the president would have been most vulnerable. I think it was during a brief stop at the American school in Busan."

"Has that event already happened?"

"Yes, they moved everything around, the timing and inside rather than outside. They've also moved up his departure tomorrow. Should be leaving shortly after you do."

"Hopefully it won't affect our departure."

"You may want to try to get out of there a little earlier."

"I'll pass that along." Clint started to write out "by the way", but remembered Buzz' use of btw. Hell, he didn't want to look like he wasn't savvy with all the texting acronyms. "BTW, Buzz, thanks for watching out for us."

"One more thing, I did see an NSA intercept in the last hour about the Busan police reporting that they believe they have arrested one of the NK agents. A man found on the street was taken directly to a hospital. With all the stuff going on, the hospital staff called the police. Don't know why, and I haven't seen any follow up. Also, I haven't seen anything that the South Koreans may have told our guys yet."

"I'll pass this along to the boss, anything else?"

"No, but one of us will stay in touch."

Clint terminated the contact and wondered what Deer and Rivers were up to. He looked at his watch. Although it was only nine thirty and he had consumed a couple cups of coffee, he wanted nothing more than to go to sleep. Must be the jet lag, he thought. It certainly seemed like he had been in Korea longer than he had.

While Clint waited, Eleanor Rivers assisted Deer in cleaning the wound to her arm. Deer declined Rivers initial offer to assist, but the woman was insistent, and Deer had given in. Why hide the obvious, she thought.

Rivers gasped when she saw the wound. Not only was the arm around the wound discolored and puffy, the wound had partially crusted over and oozed an ugly fluid from the cracks on both sides of her arm.

"Christ, Sara, you shouldn't wait until tomorrow to get this taken care of."

"Tomorrow is almost here."

When Deer removed her blouse, Rivers eyes had bounced back and forth between the long nasty gash that ran across Deer's belly an inch above the waist of her jeans and the wound on the arm. The one on the arm looked more dangerous, but the length of the one across her belly shocked her.

"I hope your job pays a lot."

"I wish," Deer said and forced a smile.

"Bullet wounds?" Rivers asked, although she knew Clint had already told her.

"Yeah, I'm getting slow in my old age."

"You know they say fifty is the new thirty," Rivers said with a smile.

"I guess the black eye doesn't help. I may look fifty, but I'm not there yet."

"Me, too."

CHAPTER 30

Busan police Sergeant Lee Lim Kwan awoke to his alarm. Six thirty in the morning, and while he knew the alarm had awakened him, he felt certain he didn't sleep at all during the night. He stood up and immediately felt nauseous. He looked at his still sleeping wife while he walked to the bathroom. What would she think of him if she knew the truth? The nausea slowly passed, but a dull headache replaced it.

He dressed in his uniform and drank a cup of coffee before leaving his house. As he closed the door to his house, he had an uneasy feeling he would never return. His hand seemed to cling to the door knob. He had to force it to let go. He drove to a spot near the tall building where he would rendezvous with the North Korean assassin.

Could he go through with this? Although his mind had gone through his options a million times over, he found himself doing so again. He should call his superiors and report what was happening. He could turn himself in, but that would ruin his life, and worse, it could endanger his family. If he let the North Korean go through with killing the American president, he would have a chance of continuing his life. Maybe he could learn to forgive himself. Maybe the assassin would miss or maybe the American leader would change his schedule. Deep down he knew that was the coward's choice, but it also seemed his only choice.

Lighter traffic than normal filled the streets this morning. The mayor had declared it a day off for all non-essential city employees and many businesses had given their employees the day off. Schools were closed for the day. The high rise building that they would be using looked quiet.

"Good morning, Sergeant," Yi Sung Minh said, surprising Lee as he approached him from behind. "Lovely day don't you think?" Yi carried an oversized briefcase in which Lee knew he had everything he needed to complete his mission.

"Yes," he replied in a voice that couldn't hide the fear that had him rattled.

"Cheer up. Everything is going to be fine."

The man must be psychotic, the policeman thought to himself, but followed him across the street. What other choice did he have?

They found the front door to the building locked.

"Not a problem, I can get us in the side door," Yi said. "Oh, here comes someone now. This should make it a lot simpler."

A young woman approached the door from the inside and opened it to leave. The two men stepped aside and held the door open after she went by. They entered the foyer and walked directly to the elevators. Once on the twenty third floor, the same one they had visited the day before, Yi walked to the apartment as though he had been going there his whole life.

Sergeant Lee wondered if Yi had remembered the key, but before he had a chance to use it, the door to the adjacent apartment opened.

"Sergeant Lee, how are you today? What brings you up here?"

Despite himself, Lee smiled as he recognized the young police officer who had only joined the force a few months earlier. Lee had been assigned to help mentor the young man and had become fond of him.

"Officer Chan, I didn't know you lived here," Lee said.

"I don't, I'm taking care of my uncle's place while he's in Seoul for the week. Better than staying with my parents," he said with a smile.

Yi interrupted the two. "I'm thinking of renting or buying this place," he motioned with his head toward the door in front of him. "Are they laid out the same?"

"I think so," the young policeman said.

"Could we take a look at it? Is there anyone else there?" Yi asked.

"We don't need to bother—"

"It's no bother, Sergeant Lee. Come look," Chan reopened the door and led the two men into his uncle's home.

"Very nice," the North Korean said. "Must be a nice view from the balcony."

"Awesome," the young man said. He walked over to the window and pointed. "Sergeant, you can see one of our precinct headquarters over there."

The older cop looked out the window. "You're right."

He heard the sound of a muffled gunshot behind him. His stomach knotted, and he forced himself to turn around in time to see the young officer collapse straight down into an unnatural position. The dead man's eyes seem to stare at him. Without knowing it, the police sergeant's hand had gone to his own service revolver.

"Don't do it," Yi snarled.

Sergeant Lee looked at Yi. "Why?" he asked and tried hard to get his emotions under control. He also moved his hand away from his own weapon.

"You know it had to be done. Now hand me your weapon and be careful how you do it. I told you that I'd let you live if you assisted me, and I plan to stick with my deal. However, if I sense any more resistance, I will kill you and then go kill the rest of your family. Do you understand? Their future rests in your hands today."

Sergeant Lee couldn't maintain eye contact and nodded his head.

Yi wanted to kill the cop, but he knew he might need him in the few hours that were left before he could complete the mission. After that, he would decide whether to kill the man or not, and he was fairly certain that his decision would leave Lee dead on the floor next to his fellow police officer.

Sergeant Lee carefully removed his police issued pistol and handed it to the assassin. The small weapon that Yi had aimed at him was almost entirely concealed in Yi's hand. He could see some sort of noise suppressor attached to the end of the barrel.

"It's a small weapon but completely lethal at this distance. I can assure you the man died without suffering."

Lee wanted to argue with him. He wanted to yell at him, to tell him that they could've simply tied the man up, but he remained silent. He knew it would be futile to try to reason with him.

Once Yi had the policeman's weapon, he put his small pistol back into his pocket. In seconds he had Lee's gun broken down into a handful of parts. He pocketed a small part and left the rest of the pieces on a coffee table. "You can put it back together after I leave. Now, let's get to work."

Over the next thirty minutes, the two went through the apartment to verify there were no security cameras or anything else of concern. Yi brewed a pot of coffee and the two men poured themselves a cup.

Yi knew he would have to keep a close eye on the policeman, but he sensed that the man was totally defeated. After he finished his mission and despite what he had said, Yi knew it would be wise to kill the man. No reason to leave any loose ends.

The balcony looked like a mirror image of the one they had seen on the adjacent apartment the day before. This one did have some furniture on it, but nothing Yi could use. Concrete walls extending up to the floor above at both ends of the balcony would provide some privacy, but Yi knew it would be unwise to stick the end of the sniper rifle out through the metal railing until the last minute or two. After having Sergeant Lee sit on a chair at the far end of the balcony, he retrieved the parts of the rifle from the briefcase and put them together.

He used the scope to find the consulate. "That's nice. They already have the podium set up in the courtyard." He moved the scope a little and studied the flag at the other end of the compound. He noted that the breeze barely moved the flag.

Yi glanced over at the policeman who looked away not willing to keep eye contact. Yes, once he had killed his target he would kill the policeman.

CHAPTER 31

Kim Moon Jin and Li Chang did not have the good fortune of someone opening the front door for them. At least, not in the manner that the young woman did for Yi Sung Minh. They found the front door of the high-rise office building locked.

"I figured the door might be locked this early," Kim said. He stepped away from the door and looked around. They would use the back entrance to break in. Fortunately, they had the presence of mind to examine the other entrances to the building the day before. A rapping on the glass door surprised him.

"What are you doing?' he snarled.

"There's a man in there, he may let us in," Li answered.

Kim hissed something that Li didn't quite understand, but Li knew it wasn't a thank you. The front door opened, and a very thin security guard looked out.

"The building's closed today," the guard said.

"What do you mean? I have work to do," Kim said.

"Where's your building pass or a letter confirming your appointment? For the last week we have been informing everyone in the building about today," the guard held his ground.

"Let me in and I will show you whatever you want." Kim took a step forward bumping into the guard.

The guard's resolve faltered a bit. He took a step backward but did not clear a way for Kim to get by.

Kim feigned exasperation and looked back and forth like he was trying to find someone to support his request. Confirming no pedestrians were nearby at this early hour, Kim stepped forward and jammed a small pistol under the guard's chin and pulled the trigger. The weapon was the same type Yi used to kill the young police lieutenant, quiet and lethal at very close range.

The guard started to collapse, but Kim caught him and kept him up.

"Help me move him."

Li quickly grabbed the man, and the two assassins moved the dead guard to a small closet at the far end of the foyer. After securing the dead man in the closet, Kim moved to the counter behind which the guards sat. He studied the computer screen on top of the counter. The screen displayed various views of the inside and outside of the building. To his surprise, in one of the boxes he saw the back entrance to the building. Yesterday he had not seen a camera anywhere around the back door. It must have been concealed. Maybe it was good after all that they didn't use the back door. He didn't say anything to Li Chang though. He didn't like the man and saw no need to telling him that he had done something right.

"Down here," Li said.

Kim looked down and saw a second processing unit or server in which he imagined the security video data was stored.

"Keep an eye out," Kim said. He unplugged the small lamp on the counter and cut the electric cord with his knife. He stripped the cut end of the cord and plugged the cord back into the outlet in the wall. He then touched the live, exposed end of the wires to the metal plate on the back of the component in the lower shelf. Sparks jumped off the end of the wire, but Kim casually pulled the cord back before repeating the task. The screen on the monitor on top of the counter flashed brightly and faded to a solid dull blue.

"Get the lamp," he ordered, and Li Chang grabbed it off the counter. Kim unplugged and handed the cord to Li. After surveying the area and seeing no signs of disturbance, they walked straight to the elevators.

"Hopefully, anyone waking by will simply believe the guard is doing something away from his post," Li said.

Kim nodded as the elevator arrived. When the doors opened, the two froze when they saw a second security guard on the elevator. As the guard started to leave the elevator, Kim pressed the small pistol against the man's side.

"Back on," he instructed.

The guard flinched but realized immediately that the man was not kidding. He stepped back into the elevator, and the two North Koreans followed.

"Turn around and face the wall. Hands up and against the wall."

The guard complied. "Just do what you all want and leave, I won't be a problem," the guard said.

Kim did not see a weapon other than a can of what looked like pepper spray on the guard. He removed it along with a radio and a cell phone, both clipped onto the man's belt.

"Do as we say and nothing will happen to you."

The guard nodded, wanting to believe what he was being told.

The three proceeded to the fifteenth floor. The found the hallway empty when they got off the elevator. Kim pushed the guard.

"Straight ahead. Do you have an access key to these offices?"

"Yes," the guard answered. His voice so choked with fear that Kim almost couldn't understand him.

Kim directed him to the office that they had checked out the day before.

"Open it."

The guard fumbled with a key chain before he managed to get the door open. Kim pushed him inside and followed him in. Once the three were inside, Kim shot the man in the back of the head. The weapon made almost no noise, and Li Chang, focused on closing the door behind him, almost tripped over the dead body.

"Get the man's key. We may need it."

Li squatted down and pulled the keys out of the dead man's hand. There were six keys in all, but he had observed a small piece of white tape on the key that the man had used to open the door. He saw that the tape had nothing written on it and supposed the tape alone signified its purpose.

"Hurry up," Kim said.

"We've got a couple of hours," Li said. When he stood up, Kim leaned into him making Li take a step back and bump against the door.

"Just do as I say when I say it," Kim said in a voice that was as cold as ice.

"Yes, sir."

Kim turned away and walked toward the office that they planned to use.

Li Chang had to hold back his desire the shoot Kim in the back. If he wasn't afraid that the man would not die, but spin around and shoot him, he would have. He hated Kim, but he was in awe of his skills as a killer and as a survivor. He followed Kim to the office and onto the balcony.

"This will do," Kim said.

He returned to the office, opened the briefcase that he had brought with him, and started to assemble the rifle. Kim liked the rifle, a Chinese clone of the Russian Dragunov sniper rifle. The smaller round that the NSG-85 used made it less effective at extreme ranges than some of the heavier sniper rifles used by the Americans and other western military services. However, his target today would be in range.

"Check all the other offices and make sure no one else is here," he said.

Li almost remarked that it was kind of late to do that. Instead he nodded and left. He guessed it was possible that someone could have been in one of the other interior offices and not heard anything. He walked the interior hallway and peered in each office. As expected, he saw no one. The last room had a number of bottles on a shelf against a side wall. Li entered the room and saw that the bottles contained a variety of alcoholic beverages.

"Johnny Walker," he said to himself and took the bottle off the shelf. He guessed the room served as a meeting room or a break room. A small refrigerator purred nearby next to a sink. He thought about looking for ice, but took a sip straight from the bottle. He grimaced as the scotch rolled over his tongue and down his throat. Looking back at the door and seeing no one, Li took another longer draw from the bottle.

Li had rarely tasted any alcoholic beverages that had not been produced in Korea. The variety of bottles on the shelf intrigued him. He decided to check in with Kim and then return to the room after Kim told him he needed nothing.

"The other offices are empty. Do you need any assistance here, or should I sit out there by the entrance to make sure no one surprises us?" Li asked.

Kim had the sniper rifle assembled and was polishing the scope with a cloth. "See if you can find some coffee and anything to eat. I think I saw a coffee maker when we first entered."

Li returned to the open reception area and saw the coffee machine. He studied it and noticed a three by five card sitting next to it with operating instructions. The machine made one cup at a time. He took the first cup to Kim along with a pack of sugar and a pack of creamer.

"Now find someplace where you won't bother me," Kim said.

Li left, pleased that he wasn't ordered to stay in the room on the off chance that Kim might need him. Of course, he knew the "great" Kim needed no one. He wanted to go straight to the break room, but decided he should have a cup of coffee first. It wouldn't be wise to get drunk before the assassination succeeded. He could take the bottle with him when he left.

Li made himself some coffee and found a comfortable, stuffed chair to sit in. He took a sip of coffee before leaning back and closing his eyes.

A violent kick to his shin awoke him.

"Wake up!" Kim hissed.

Li lurched to his feet. "Sorry, I must have fallen asleep."

"It's almost time. Once I shoot the target, we will have to leave. There will be no time for me to wake you up. I can have no interruption. Anyone comes in from now on, deal with it. Do not bother me. Kill whoever it is."

"Yes, sir."

"Another screw up and you will find yourself like your friend over there." Kim pointed to the dead security guard.

Li nodded. He wanted to say the guard was not his friend, but Kim knew that. He also wanted to tell Kim that he, too, had a weapon that could kill.

"This should be over in less than a half hour. No more screw ups."

Li watched Kim return to the office. He looked down and noticed his hands were shaking. Kim didn't need him after the mission was accomplished. For the first time, he started to wonder if he would die today. Li returned to the break room and took a bottle of Jim Beam off the shelf. He took a sip and noticed right away that it went down a lot smoother than the scotch. He took a second sip and studied his watch. A third of the bottle and twenty minutes later he had made his decision. Kim and Yi would take their shots in exactly twelve minutes.

Li walked as steadily as he could to the office and then to the balcony where Kim was already in position.

"Everything okay?" he asked.

"Yes, leave me alone," Kim answered as expected.

Li Chang returned to the break room, stuffed a few miniature bottles of vodka into his pockets, and walked to the outer door of the offices. He left, locking the office door and headed straight for the elevators.

Chapter 32

"Good morning," Clint said when Eleanor Rivers opened her eyes. He brushed the hair out of her face.

"You sure we can't stay here all day?" she asked.

"It would be nice, but we'll have a few days together in Guam."

"You won't run off and leave me as soon as we get there?"

"No way," Clint said. He climbed out of bed and headed into the bathroom.

Rivers stretched out in the bed and yawned. She was pleased that Sara's arrival to her house hadn't disrupted the sleeping arrangements. Her thoughts of Clint's co-worker caused her to get up and grab her bathrobe. She left her room to check on her wounded guest and found her still asleep in one of the guest rooms. Rivers paused at the door until she was certain that she could see the subtle movements of her guest breathing.

She returned to her bedroom and found Clint slipping into his jeans.

"Sara seems to be sleeping well."

"Good. I hope you slept well, too."

"Ha! If I remember right I had to beg you to finally let me sleep," she said.

"I think you have that reversed. I tried to be a gentleman." He smiled, drew her close, and kissed her.

"See, there you go again, trying to take advantage of me." She gently pushed him away and entered the bathroom, closing the door behind her.

Clint looked at his watch and saw that it was nearly eight in the morning. "What time do we need to leave for the airport?"

"About an hour before the flight," Rivers replied, "but I have to run by the old office this morning to get my passport. My last trip out of the country was with a few members of the company's board. When we returned we went straight to the offices, and I locked my passport in my office safe there."

"Ok," but it really wasn't. He didn't expect this extra trip away from the house and only hours before the flight. He told himself to let it go, but he couldn't shake the suspicions that drifted in from the back of his mind.

He finished dressing and went to check on Deer. He found her awake and sitting on her bed. She was scratching the top of her head with her eyes half closed. "This would be a great picture for Facebook," Clint said.

She looked up at him and grimaced. "Don't even think of it."

"Are you going to make it to Guam?"

"Yes, but we better be leaving today. How are you doing?"

"Fine, but Rivers just mentioned she needs to run to her old office this morning to get her passport."

"Are you uncomfortable with that? Think she's getting away from here so the police can come get us?"

"I just didn't expect it, and this late in the game it does make me wonder."

"Well, you can wonder away, but it's not like we gave her a lot of time to plan for an international trip. I doubt if we need to worry, but you can always ride along with her. At least that will mess up her being alone or us being together."

Clint nodded. "Are you going to need any help getting dressed?"

"I think I can manage. Go find us some coffee," she waved the back of her hand at him as though she was brushing him away.

Clint went to the kitchen and was about to start a search for the coffee when Rivers entered.

"No hired help today. Just me, so I hope your breakfast desires don't go beyond a fried egg and some toast."

"Coffee is about all I need and maybe a piece of any leftover dessert from last night. That was really good."

"Perfect. I can make that happen. Did you check on Sara?"

"Yes, she asked for coffee, too."

Rivers pulled a plate out of the refrigerator that contained the remains of the prior night's dessert and handed it to Clint.

"Forks are in that drawer. Eat all you want, because what we don't eat goes into the trash before we leave."

Clint sat down on one of the stools that lined the island in the kitchen. Rivers set a mug of coffee in front of him.

"Thanks. Now that we are leaving, I'm beginning to wish I could stay with you here for a few more days," he said. "I like being spoiled."

"You're easy to spoil. I'll be back in a jiff," she said and walked out of the kitchen with a mug of coffee that he imagined she was taking to Deer.

Rivers found Deer sitting on a chair in the bedroom and thought the woman looked like she could use a full day at the spa. "How are you feeling this morning?" She handed Deer the cup of coffee.

"Wrinkled, dirty clothes, bad hair, headache, feeling old, but besides that I'm trying real hard not to feel sorry for myself. Otherwise, I'm fine, and I do appreciate all that you are doing for us. Believe me, I will try to find a way to pay you back."

"Not necessary. And I hope you don't mind my saying so, but since you're the reason Clint came to Korea, you've paid me back already."

Deer half smiled. "You know he's leaving," she said gently.

"Oh, I know. In fact, I wouldn't want to keep him, so knowing that he will be leaving makes it easier. My life had started to get boring and lonely. I began to feel sorry for myself despite knowing that for many years I had led a life of travel, fun, and extravagance that most women would die for. He and all this have brought a little excitement back into my life."

"Still, I can't help but feel indebted to you." Deer took a sip of coffee and looked into Eleanor Rivers eyes. She didn't think Clint's concern that this woman might still turn them in had any credibility.

"Let me help you with your hair," Rivers said and removed a brush from a nearby drawer. Deer wanted to say she wasn't helpless, but didn't resist as Rivers calmly stroked her hair. What woman didn't like to have her hair brushed?

"Are you going to need any help getting dressed?"

Deer answered that she needed some help getting into her sky-blue tee shirt that she was going to wear under her lightweight jacket. The jacket would serve to hide the wound to her arm. They both acknowledged the bruising to her face had taken on a dull bluish green tone and would require a little extra makeup to cover it.

Rivers helped Deer with her shirt and noticed the wound had not bled through the bandage wrap that they had put on her arm the night before.

"Should we change the bandage one more time before we leave?" Rivers asked.

"No, I don't think we need to. You did a good job last night, and it looks intact and clean. I don't think it'll hurt anything to wait until we get to Guam this afternoon."

Rivers returned to the kitchen to find Clint finishing off the tray of desserts. "You were hungry. I thought you said you couldn't eat the whole plate?" She took Clint's cup to the counter to refill it as he finished chewing.

"After I had one, I knew I could eat them all, so I put a couple on a plate and left it over there so it would stay out of reach." He nodded with his head at the far side of the counter.

"Well, I don't want any, so I wouldn't have cared, but Sara may want some. She should be down in a minute."

Rivers sat down next to Clint and the two again discussed the house, living in Busan, the American community in the area, and other benign topics. A couple times they wondered out loud if they should check on Deer, or Sara as they both referred to her, since she seemed to be taking a long time.

Finally, Deer entered the kitchen and greeted them both.

"Hey, you look a lot better today," Clint said.

"I made a real effort not to look like the walking dead when we go through security today."

"Well, you do look better, and I hate to disappoint you, but we shouldn't be walking through any checkpoints. I hope they'll send someone out to the plane. That's how they've done it in the past," Rivers said.

"Then I hope that's how they'll do it today. Any changes in plans yet?" Deer asked.

"We may have access to a wheelchair. I know you don't need it, but it may help us attract less suspicion if I wheel you out to the plane," Clint suggested.

"Ugh, I hate playing the old invalid," Deer said, "but, we'll see."

"I mentioned to Clint that I need to run by my office to get my passport. It's in the opposite direction from the airport, so I'll do it before we leave to go to the airport. Traffic should be light today as most of the offices, schools, and shops are closed. I think we can avoid any of the roads shut down for the day."

"Do you mind if I ride along?" Clint asked.

"Not at all," she said, but her eyes looked at him in a manner that Clint interpreted as questioning why.

"Eleanor, how long will you be staying in Guam?" Clint asked, changing the topic for the moment.

"How long will you be staying?"

"I could stand a few days on the beach. That is, as long as I have some company."

"I thought I'd spend three nights there before coming back. That would give me two full days on the beach and maybe do some snorkeling. The water is beautiful there. Have you done any snorkeling?" she asked Clint.

"I'd love to learn," Clint said, even though he was a pretty good snorkeler.

"No one worry about me," Deer chimed in.

"We'll visit, of course," Clint said. "After they amputate that arm of yours, they'll probably keep you in the hospital a few days. You know, though, I think I'm off the hook once I deliver you into the doctor's hands."

"Not funny and nobody is cutting off my arm. I'm dreading what they may have to do, but amputation is not going to be one of their options."

"Surely the wound isn't that bad," Rivers said, reaching out with her hand to touch Deer's hand. At the same time, she gave Clint a look that left little doubt that his remark was out of line.

The topic turned to other things to do in Guam, and after about twenty minutes, Rivers excused herself to make a few phone calls.

"Have you heard anything from D.C.?" Clint asked.

"Only a short text saying there wasn't any new news. I'll let them know when we're about to take off, and then we should be home free. Eleanor has invited me back to tour Korea. She offered to be my guide, and I may take her up on that. It's a beautiful country, but I would definitely need a guide. Funny, here we are trying to get out of here as soon as possible, and I'm already thinking about coming back."

"This is not a very normal visit," Clint said.

"No, it isn't. Remind me to tell Buzz that the next time I think I need to take on one of these missions, to not let me."

"I already have," Clint said with a grin.

CHAPTER 33

Clint sat in the back seat with Rivers as her driver drove them into the city. Despite her comment that traffic would be light, the street they were on was busy. However, they didn't encounter any real congestion and finally pulled to a stop in front of a tall office building.

"You can wait in the car, Clint. No need for you to have to go in with me."

"That's okay. It'll be good to stretch my legs."

Clint saw the look of subtle suspicion cross Rivers' face. He chose to ignore it rather than say anything.

They found the entrance locked and Rivers peered in through the glass. "There should be a security guard in there, but I can't see him. Not a problem, I have a key." She reached into her purse and pulled out a set of keys. Using one she opened the door, and the two entered the large foyer.

They headed toward the elevators, but Clint paused when they passed the counter that served as the security guard's station. He smelled the faint odor of ozone. Mostly a distraction, it did cause him to study the area around the counter where he saw a small smear of blood on the side of the counter stand near the floor. His eyes seemed to work on instinct, and he found a few more drops of blood nearby in front of a door that he thought might lead into a closet. A few more drops led toward the building's front doors.

"Clint?" Rivers called from the elevators.

As she stood there, the elevator doors opened and a man came out walking by Rivers. He took three steps and stopped, staring at Clint.

"I think I'll stay down here, Eleanor. Please, go on."

Rivers thought the tone of his voice had changed. She felt his comment was more of an order than a suggestion. The elevator door had already tried to close and she was holding it open. She stepped into the elevator and the door closed behind her. A bit confused, she could ask him what was going on when she returned in a few minutes.

Most people wouldn't have made the identification so quickly. After all they had only seen each other that once, but both Clint and Li Chang were not most people.

Weaponless, Clint tried to weigh the odds. He recognized the man as the individual he saw running at him with the intent of stopping him from getting into the taxi near the side door of the hotel.

There was too much distance between them for Clint to do much. If the man had a gun, he was toast.

Li Chang's mind, on the other hand, went in a totally different direction. A warm feeling spread through him. The Jim Beam was only partially to blame. Fortune must have brought the big American to him to help him make good with his escape from Kim and the rest of those who would otherwise be looking for him soon.

"You better hurry if you want to save your president. Go to room 1512. A man there will shoot him in less than five minutes. You better hurry, American." Li tossed Clint a set of keys before raising the small handgun in his right hand pointing it upward in a display to show that he was armed and walked out of the building.

Li Chang couldn't believe his luck. Let this big American who had already defeated a half dozen or so of Li's associates confront the invincible Kim. It would be a battle worth watching, but he couldn't stay to enjoy it. No matter who won, it would provide him with cover while he disappeared into anonymity.

Clint might have been more stunned if he hadn't seen the small blood trail or didn't already suspect that these assassins were targeting the president. However, he never anticipated what had just happened. He sent Rivers ahead to keep her out of whatever mayhem he anticipated would result from a confrontation with the North Korean. Not only was there no confrontation, he thought he heard the North Korean giggling as he left the building. Clint's thoughts of Rivers faded, and he rushed to the elevators hoping one of the other elevators would be waiting there for him.

Clint didn't know where the president would be in the next five minutes, but imagined that wherever he would be the shooter could see him from the fifteenth floor. He knew a good sniper could hit someone over a mile away. A half circle with the radius of a mile took up a lot of territory, even in a big city like Busan. Clint's luck held, and the elevator door to his left opened. He jumped in and pressed the button for the fifteenth floor.

In the elevator, he studied the key ring in an attempt to find a master key. Although the key ring held several keys, the number had to only be a fraction of the total number of doors in the building. One had to be the master key. He noticed one key had a small piece of white tape on it. The tape had been there for some time signifying something that its owner wanted to use to identify the key's significance whenever he needed it to.

"I bet it's you," Clint remarked to the key.

He didn't have a weapon, nor did he have time to contact someone who could get the authorities here in time to stop the assassin. If the five minute warning had been correct, then there was less than four minutes now. Clint had no choice but to try to stop the assassination attempt by himself. He would have to find something to use along the way.

The elevator moved like an express to the fifteenth floor. Clint was out and had taken a handful of steps before he realized he was going in the wrong direction. He reversed direction and sprinted down the hall. Whoever was inside wouldn't think twice about hearing the door open as the person would think it was his partner coming back. But what if there were more than one person in the office?

"Damn," Clint muttered but pressed on. He almost ran by the door. He pushed the key into the door and turned it. The door clicked open.

Relieved, Clint stepped in and stopped when he saw the dead security guard. Looking around, he noticed he had entered not one office but a space that contained a reception area along with a number of desks for what he supposed to be the administrative staff. Against the far wall, he could see three separate rooms, and more were likely down the hall that ran off to the right out of sight.

The guard didn't have a gun and he discounted using the pepper spray. Instead, Clint grabbed a glass paperweight off a nearby desk. The size of a softball and solid, it would serve as fair weapon if his throw was accurate, or if he could smash it against someone's head. He glanced into the offices starting with the one to his far left. Moving as quietly as he could, he finally saw a man prone on the balcony floor in the fifth office. He couldn't see the entire body, but he saw enough to know what he was doing.

Kim Moon Jin sensed more than heard the movement at the door that led out onto the balcony. The movement initially annoyed him, and he wanted to yell at Li to stay away, but almost simultaneously, he felt something was wrong. His target had not appeared yet, so he took his eyes away from scope and glanced back at the door.

Almost nothing surprised this North Korean, but seeing the tall American throwing what looked like a shiny ball at him from only a few yards away made it into that rare category. The surprise almost allowed the glass paperweight to hit him in his face. At the last millisecond, Kim jerked his head back, and the paperweight smashed into the stock of the rifle with enough force to crack it and knock it out of Kim's hands.

Clint charged the North Korean knowing he had to close the

gap before the man had a chance to pull another weapon out of a pocket or hidden holster. The man rolled away from Clint with a speed more like a cat or a mongoose than a human. The assassin made it back to his feet and pulled a small pistol out of somewhere. He almost had the weapon up and aimed when Clint crashed into him and crushed him against the concrete wall that separated this balcony from the next. Both men grunted. Clint successfully ripped the pistol from the man's hand.

The North Korean collapsed to the floor, and Clint took a half step backward, intending to get a better grip on the weapon and shoot the man while he was stunned. This time, however, Kim surprised him by kicking Clint behind the knee with one foot while using his other leg to trip Clint and make him fall backwards.

A number of things went through Clint's mind as he fell backwards. The first being "How the hell did he do that?" His next few thoughts focused on keeping himself alive. He didn't want his head to hit the hard floor and used both arms to help break the fall. In doing so, the pistol bounced out of Clint's hand and through the railing to the ground far below. He saw the Korean coil and lunge at him. The man had something in his right hand that glimmered in the morning sun.

Clint rolled to his right anticipating the man would grip him with his left hand and then try to stab him with the knife. He felt the man clutch at his shirt as he finished his roll. Clint got his feet under him and swung his left arm around blindly. Fortune was with him as he struck the Korean's arm knocking the hand with the knife away at the instant the knife made contact with his shirt.

He jabbed with his right fist, hitting Kim in the face and knocking him back a step. The blow did little more than put the North Korean off balance, but Clint needed time to get a grip on the man's wrist. He had a considerable size advantage and had little doubt that he had an advantage in strength. Once he had successfully grabbed the man's wrist, he went immediately to the man's throat with his right hand. Clint believed he had the fight under control.

What Clint didn't realize was that Kim wasn't merely a great fighter, he was in a class of his own. Kim's mind somehow had the ability to turn every situation into an opportunity. As soon as the American's hand grabbed his throat, Kim threw his legs up and around the American's right side. He used the American's strength against him, knowing that the American would either let go or adjust his grip. He sensed the grip loosen on his throat and used his left hand to further break the grip.

However, dislodging Clint's grip on his throat or his knife hand was not the primary purpose of Kim's maneuver. As he swung his legs up in the air behind the American's back, in one swift motion he shot his left leg over Clint's head and under his chin. He then locked his left foot under his right leg positioned behind Clint's neck. With all his might he tightened his legs.

Whatever advantage Clint thought he had vanished. At the same time, he knew his opponent fit in a category that he thought he would never personally have to face. Despite all of his own training and experience, and the fact that he had become as good as any martial arts trainer he ever hired, Clint always knew there had to be a handful of others scattered around the world who were better than him. Unfortunately, he was now in a fight to the death with one of them.

Clint had tucked his chin when the leg tightened around his throat, but the leg seemed to ignore it edging down and then back up under the chin in one fluid motion. Clint let go of the man's throat knowing that he couldn't let go of the man's knife hand. With his free right hand, Clint started to grab the man's leg to pull it away from his throat.

The North Korean bucked up and his free hand went for Clint's eyes. Instinctively, Clint grabbed the man's arm at the elbow and shoved it away.

For a moment it seemed to Clint that time was frozen. He stood still feeling his oxygen being cut off. Both his hands trapped because he didn't dare let go of this man who literally hung from him. He slipped his right hand up the man's armpit and pushed as hard as he could. Despite his strength, this did little besides put a lot of stress on the Korean's frame. Clint didn't have enough strength to tear the man's body apart, and without the use of his hands he had no way to loosen the grip his opponent's legs had on his throat.

Kim realized what the big American was doing and felt the stress his own body was being put through. Substantial pain shot through various parts of his own body, but Kim knew his body would hold and that the American wouldn't last much longer without oxygen. Before he blacked out, the American would release his grip to try again to break the choke hold. He had the strength to do it, but Kim would do serious damage to the man's eyes with his free hand and stab him with the knife if his right hand came loose. He knew where the arteries ran close to the skin, and if the man didn't suffocate to death he would most certainly bleed to death. He stared into the American's widening eyes.

Clint looked back into the North Korean's eyes. What did he see in them? Contempt, hate, no, he believed it was sheer determination. Clint began to feel the lack of oxygen despite his desperate gasps for air. At this point in the struggle, Clint stood fairly upright with his opponent's legs choking him and the rest of the man almost perpendicular out to his right.

Like a circus contortionist, the Korean's torso tried to twist at the waist to get even more leverage to his legs and further tighten their hold on Clint's neck. Kim would tolerate the American's attempt to push him away. In fact, he took advantage of Clint's arm to get this additional leverage.

Unexpectedly, the American swung Kim's head and most of his body out over the railings. If he thought this might frighten

Kim into letting him go, he had made a mistake. Kim had no intention of undoing the choke hold until the man was down and out. He didn't believe the American intended to send them both over the balcony to their deaths below.

Clint tightened his grip and started shaking his opponent before moving a step to his right. He knew he had to do something in the next ten or so seconds and hoped the man didn't expect his next move. Suddenly, Clint swung the man's upper body to his right and smashed his head into the outer corner of the concrete wall between the balconies.

Kim realized too late what was happening and his head collided with the wall before he could break the man's hold on his arm. The blow hurt, but he forced his mind to stay focused on maintaining his choke hold. He tucked his chin as deep into his right shoulder as he could to help minimize the subsequent blow that he now knew was coming.

Clint swung the man's head into the wall a second time and knew immediately that it had less of an impact. Almost in a panic, he swung the man around in a wide arc in the opposite direction and smashed the North Korean's head into the large window of the sliding glass door, while throwing all his own weight into the collision. He hoped that the window might break, but despite the loud impact, the thick safety glass held. Turning to his right he raised the assassin's head as high as he could, before bringing it down and hitting the back of the man's neck on the top cross bar of the balcony railings. Simultaneously, Clint drove his arm much like a running back in football might stiff arm a defensive back to do extra damage to his opponent's neck and head.

Clint started to see stars and felt a blackout coming when he twirled the man like a rag doll back into the window. Once more, the window shuddered as the collision with the man's head produced a loud bang, but the window somehow held. Clint dropped to one knee holding the impression of a rag doll in his mind. It took a second or two before Clint comprehended that it wasn't just an impression. He had turned the North Korean killer into a rag doll. He no longer felt the man's legs around his throat. Clint sucked air into his lungs.

The North Korean had fallen from him, although Clint couldn't remember that happening. The man's leg moved and startled Clint out of his momentary haze. Clint reached over and lifted the small knife off the floor next to the man's hand. Lifting the man's head while keeping his face toward the floor, Clint sliced the man's throat and then backed away before the blood could get on him.

Clint inhaled and fought to get his pulse under control. After a few seconds, he stood up and checked himself for any obvious injuries. He studied the area around him and made sure he hadn't dropped anything. He removed the scope from the rifle and put it in the receptionist's desk drawer. No one could hit a distant target without the scope, and he knew the police would find it. Picking up the glass paperweight, he first wiped off any fingerprints he may have left on it and then placed it back where he had found it. Surprisingly, the glass ball did not show any signs of being damaged.

He knew he had to leave. He had no reason to suspect that anything had happened to Rivers, but he would feel better once the two of them left the building. Once in the car, he could contact Buzz or Dolly, and they could get an anonymous tip to the Busan police. On the way to the elevator Clint did his best to straighten out his clothing and hide any obvious signs of a struggle.

"There you are," Eleanor Rivers said when she saw Clint get out of the elevator. She looked at him and frowned. "What happened to you?"

"A little distraction. We should leave," Clint could tell his voice sounded hoarse.

"When I came down here you were gone. I went out to the car

but you weren't there. We thought you might be in the restroom, so I came back into wait." She still looked at him questionably. "What is going on, Clint? Is this why you wanted to come with me?"

She handed him a tissue that she pulled out of her purse and pointed to a spot on his face under his right eye.

Clint took the tissue and her hand giving her a slight tug toward the exit. "I'll tell you in the car."

The two walked to the car and Rivers told her driver to take them home. The car pulled away from the curb, and Rivers took the unused tissue out of Clint's hand and dabbed at an area on his cheek. She pulled it away and showed him.

"Blood? Mine?"

"That's a strange question, but yes. Someone scratched you, plus your face was flushed when you came out of the elevator. It's still a little flush. Your hair is a mess, and I noticed when you got into the car that you have a tear in your shirt."

"I wasn't fooling around on you, if that's what you think," Clint joked.

That brought a smile to River's face. "Seriously, you knew that man who came out of the elevator, didn't you?"

"Not by name, but I did recognize him as one the North Koreans who have been chasing Sara and me."

"Did he do that to you? Where did he go? Should we call the police? If he's North Korean we need to do something?"

"Please, Eleanor, I'll explain it, but we must leave for Guam today. Any personal contact with the authorities will only delay us and cause more problems. We'll make sure the local authorities know to go to your building this morning, too. You don't need to be dragged into this anymore than we've already done to you."

Rivers turned her head away with obvious disappointment. She had no idea what had happened in the short time Clint had disappeared and didn't think much had, but his holding back information from her after all she had done and planned to do for him irritated her.

"I feel like canceling the plane. If you can't trust me by now," she said without turning her head away from the window.

"When we get back to your house, I'll tell you everything that happened. It will save me from telling it twice," he said.

She turned back to look at him, and he tried to smile his way through the disappointment she had for his making her wait.

"We'll also make sure the police are told to get over there right away. I have to do that, too," he said.

She looked at him for a few seconds, but then turned back to the window. "Did you know that man would be there? Is that why you wanted to go with me?"

"No. I had no idea, and I was more surprised he didn't kill the two of us right then and there."

"What?" Rivers turned her head to face him again. "Are you teasing me now?"

"Afraid not."

Rivers didn't want to believe him, but somehow, she knew he was telling her the truth. The thought that a few minutes earlier she had stood next to a North Korean killer filled her mind with all sorts of questions. Her imagination brought up visions that reminded her of her teenage dreams about the boogeyman.

"You didn't have to tell me that," she said. The irony of her own remark and her anger caused Rivers to wrap her arm around Clint's and squeeze.

They rode the rest of the way in relative silence.

CHAPTER 34

Yi Sung Minh made a comment that might have been "show time" if he were an American. Sergeant Lee Lim Kwan heard the remark and knew it meant that Yi, lying prone a few feet in front of him with his sniper rifle aimed at a location within the American consulate compound, had located his target.

A mile away, Lee couldn't even be sure if he could see the consulate with his naked eye. Despite his amazement that someone could actually hit a target at this distance, he knew the man on the floor of the balcony intended to do just that. Lee stepped over Yi and moved over to the other end of the balcony.

"Stay still," Yi snarled taking his eyes off the target for a second. He glanced at Lee and then at the watch he had fastened to one of the rails on the balcony. Less than a minute to go. He thought he might take the shot one second early so he could claim the kill. He wanted to see his round make contact and then continue watching as the round from Kim's rifle hit the target a second or two later. In that second before Kim's round would impact the target, he didn't think the president's body would react or move very far. He wanted to describe to his superiors how both rounds impacted with the target and how he witnessed life slipping away from the President of the United States.

"Come on," he whispered as his target paused in front of three people, each wanting to shake his hand. The rest of the small crowd remained seated in the chairs put out onto the patio. The chairs had been expected but were not there yesterday. No matter, they wouldn't interfere with the shot.

His eye went to the watch. Twenty seconds left. He would check the wind one more time and then count down the seconds in his head. He would have to keep his eye focused on the target through the scope after that and concentrate on his breathing and finally the trigger pull. He had already made slight adjustments to the scope due to the soft breeze. He saw from the flag on the compound a minute earlier that the wind had not changed in the last ten minutes. He glanced one final time back at the flag.

Sergeant Lee felt the nausea in his belly and the sweat now running down his forehead. He also felt the butt of the small caliper pistol he kept in the ankle holster. He had only worn the ankle holster once or twice before in his entire time with the police. It wasn't exactly condoned in the regulations. Somehow, his subconscious knew this would be his decision today, even if he hadn't actually acknowledged it until now.

The policeman thought he heard Yi mutter seven then six before he stood up and fired three rounds in rapid succession into Yi's back. Yi managed to start to roll to his left, but only succeeded in giving Lee an open shot to his chest. When this fourth round struck, it penetrated Yi's heart, killing the man instantly.

Lee took his phone out of his pocket and called his office. He smiled when he heard the voice of another young police officer whom he had once mentored at the other end of the line.

"Kitty," he said knowing that it was nickname given to her by the other young officers in her recruiting class. He would not normally address her this way, but this was not a normal day, and his days as a policeman might soon be over.

"I want to report a homicide with two people dead with one being the murderer." He paused while she asked a question. "Yes, I killed an assassin. Now, no more questions, this is a lot bigger than a simple murder. It involves the attempted assassination of the city's guest of honor today."

She didn't stop him to clarify who, and he continued talking. By the time he had hung up, Lee had told her most of the pertinent details she would need to set in motion a proper response. He had not told her about his past or why he was there in the apartment. He would open up but only to the right individuals and not until he felt certain that what he had to tell could be kept confidential. He knew at some point it would all come out and he would be exposed, but he would do what he could to delay that from happening.

For a moment after he had shot the North Korean, Lee considered leaving the apartment and walking away. The dead police officer on the floor inside the apartment prevented him from doing that. He sat on the couch not far from the dead officer and said a prayer, asked his dead colleague for forgiveness, and waited for the police response.

It didn't take long. The first two patrolmen arrived in less than five minutes. They offered to help secure the scene and didn't ask any questions. The more in-depth police response arrived twenty minutes later. Lee pointed out main elements of the crime scenes to the group and emphasized the significance of the sniper rifle. He didn't attempt to elaborate on the time line of events leaving a gap in his briefing wide enough for even the dullest of investigators to realize something didn't smell right.

The lead investigator, a man Lee had known for years pulled him into a private room and demanded to know what was going on.

"Sir, in a few minutes I will answer all your questions."

"I don't want to wait --"

"Sir," one of the more junior investigators interrupted them. He stood in the doorway, and Lee could see the arm of a second man standing just out of sight next to him. The man squeezed through the door way and entered the room, closing the door behind him.

Both men in the room recognized the newcomer as the second-in-command of the Korean National Police division located in Busan. Just as the Busan city police force was second only to Seoul's in size, the KNP presence in Busan was the second largest contingent in the country. While the KNP technically didn't have any control over the city police, his presence had to be respected.

"Excuse me," Sergeant Lee said to his Busan police co-worker, "but I requested Captain Sool's presence. You may know that he has close contacts in our country's security services. While I have something important to confess to both of you, I need to make sure everything I say can be kept secret until the government is sure they have wrapped up all the other North Koreans who have infiltrated our country with the intent of assassinating the United States President. And, since I've heard nothing about the president being shot, I'm assuming someone's been able to stop the other shooter." Despite what the North Korean Yi had thought, Sergeant Lee had overheard a comment made by one of the other North Koreans about there being two shooters.

Both men let what Lee told them sink in before speaking.

Captain Sool spoke first. "What do you know of the infiltration? How do you know they are targeting the American leader? How many North Koreans are here in Busan?"

"You apparently haven't been out to the balcony yet," Lee said.

Sool glanced back and forth at both men. "Wait right here for a second," he said and hurried out of the room.

"You know you shouldn't have contacted him. This is a murder scene in the city of Busan."

Lee nodded. "I imagine he will wish I never contacted you before the morning is out, too, but I agree with your assessment at this point. I never considered not contacting our department. Unfortunately, this matter goes beyond what has happened here."

"Have you been working for Sool on this?"

"I wish I had been, but no," Lee said.

Sool returned and interrupted their conversation.

"Tell me, who is he and where was he aiming? Who was his target?" Sool demanded.

"If you check you'll see the weapon has a good line of sight to the American consulate where their president may still be speaking for all I know. He came here to kill the president, but despite all my past mistakes and cowardice, I could not let him."

"You knew him?" Sool asked.

"I met him only two days ago."

The pieces started falling together in Sool's mind. He took the city police officer in charge of the scene by the arm and walked him to the door. "Please order your men to not say anything about what they see or hear today to anyone other than what is necessary to document the investigation of the two homicides."

The lead detective nodded. "I agree. Will you make all necessary contacts within the government?"

"I will. I will also have to take Sergeant Lee with me when we leave."

"I will have to advise my superiors."

"I suggest you contact the chief directly. Tell him I requested you skip the rest of the chain. He will understand. I, too, will have to contact my chief." Sool sent a short text to his office instructing that an investigative team be sent to his location. The specific team he requested would let his office know that this matter dealt with the North Korean infiltration that had recently grabbed the federal government's attention.

The two men began their preliminary interview of Lee. The real interrogation would come later, but both men knew the importance of letting the man talk if he was willing to do so before he hired a lawyer or clammed up on his own.

Lee began by requesting immediate protection for his family. Without that he would not say a word. Both men agreed to his request with all three knowing the final approval would have to be made at a higher level. Lee knew he would have to repeat his story over and over again in the next week or two but wasn't concerned. He would tell the truth. Other than the events of the last couple of days, he had very little to confess.

In fact, for the first time in a long time, Sergeant Lee Lim Kwan felt patriotic, and it felt good.

CHAPTER 35

Deer, Rivers, and Clint sat around the small kitchen table. Rivers had not offered coffee or anything else to the two. She wanted answers.

"We ran into the people who have been chasing you, and I guess me, too," Clint said. He noticed Deer's eyes jump to Rivers. "We're fine, but it had its moments."

"I didn't know anything was even going on until Clint came out of the elevator. I wasn't involved in anything other than going to my office and getting my passport. However, I need to know what happened in my building."

"I asked Eleanor to wait for an explanation until we got back here. I didn't want to go through the whole thing twice."

"I don't need to know who you guys really are, or why you are here, or what agency employs you. But things are different now. I need to know what happened in my building. There are security cameras in the building, and I don't need to be surprised by a visit by someone from the Korean government."

"Agreed," Deer said. "We'll need you to sign a secrecy agreement later. I should have mentioned that yesterday. Will that be okay?"

"Of course."

"As I think I mentioned before," Clint began, "I had no expectation of encountering anyone this morning. I recognized the man who got off the elevator as one of the men who had been following us. For a moment, I thought he was going to kill us both. That was why I told you to get into the elevator. What he did, however, totally surprised me."

For the next five minutes, Clint described what had happened that morning. When he mentioned that he discovered a North

Korean on an office balcony intent on assassinating the president, Rivers' eyes widened.

"How were you able to stop him? Shouldn't we call the police before he gets away?"

"When I mentioned that I had stopped him, I'm referring to a more permanent stoppage. He didn't give me a choice. Believe me, for a few moments there I thought it was going to be me dead up there on the balcony, not him."

"You're sure he was targeting the president?" Deer asked.

"Fairly certain."

"Send the info home and have them get it to right people here immediately. The North Koreans may have a Plan B."

"On it now," Clint said. He stood up and started texting on his phone while he walked out of the room.

Rivers felt better now that these two had started the process to get word to the Korean authorities. What made the bigger impression on her, though, was that the tone in which this woman she knew as Sara spoke to Clint gave her the impression that Sara was in charge. She hadn't barked an order, but rather spoke in a tone that assumed authority. Not that it mattered, but she found it interesting. Never hurt to have a woman in charge, she thought.

"Was this why you came to Korea, to prevent an assassination?" Rivers asked.

"It's complicated, believe me, but the simple answer is yes."

"So whatever you've done in trying to prevent an assassination angered the North Koreans. So what, they are after you in retaliation?"

Deer reflected for a second on the past couple of days. "In essence, that's correct. The irony of everything is that we had apparently accomplished very little. If they would have left us alone, Clint might not have ever recognized the North Korean this morning, and he may never have sent Clint up to stop the assassination attempt."

"How interesting, but why would he do that? Why betray his country?"

"Who knows? What's more interesting to me is how Clint's chance encounter with you yesterday is what may have resulted in saving the life of the president."

"So being a lonely old, I mean middle age woman might have its purposes after all," Rivers said with a grin. "And here I thought my motivation was much more carnal in nature than patriotic."

Her remark brought a grin to Deer's face. "My suggestion is that if you ever get questioned by the authorities, either Korean or American, about any of this, you should be truthful about everything you have done, to include having us stay here and your trip to get your passport. Just keep the conversations you've had with the two of us to yourself. If they press you on why you helped us, stick to your real motivation."

"That won't be hard, and I don't really know anything but what you've told me. I think that's called hearsay in the legal world."

"Excuse me," Clint reappeared in the doorway that led out of the kitchen. "Eleanor, can I get you to write down the address of the building we were in."

CHAPTER 36

The driver drove the car onto the tarmac and came to a stop next to a sleek jet that sat alone at this far end of the airfield. Other small private or charter aircraft sat parked a couple hundred yards to the east. An airport security vehicle and a maintenance truck had already parked near the plane. Clint could see a number of larger commercial aircraft taxiing at the other end of the long runway.

A man wearing dark slacks and a white shirt that appeared to have something embroidered above his heart walked toward them.

"Our pilot," Rivers said. She opened her car door and stepped out. "Come on out and say hello," she said.

"Ms. Rivers, I'm glad you all got here," the pilot said. "This guy's really impatient. They sent him out because he's fairly junior would be my guess. Something big is going on in the city, and he was in the process of telling me he was needed back wherever. He wanted us to process through the main terminal, and that would take at least an hour besides being a real pain in the neck."

"Let me go talk to him with you," Rivers said. "Clint, Sara let me have your passports and maybe we can get this done right now. If you would stay here, so he can see each of you."

She and the pilot walked over to the Customs officer and a second man standing next to him. Both men smiled and bowed slightly as Rivers approached. Their conversation was short and ended with the second man stamping something onto the three passports Rivers had handed him. They all shook hands before the two Customs officials returned to their vehicle. Rivers waved at them as they left. After the car departed, she and the pilot turned and signaled for Clint and Sara to board the plane.

Rivers took a quick glance at Sara's passport. She read the name, Ginger Bond. For a second, she thought she had discovered Sara's real name. She had no nefarious motivation for looking, it was simply curiosity, and confirming that Sara wasn't a real name felt somewhat satisfying. However, she had only taken a couple steps toward the plane when the last name jumped out at her. Bond? No way. A secret agent named Bond? That was one for fiction spy thrillers. She openly grinned, acknowledging to herself that she might never know Ginger's or Sara's real name.

A second man, the co-pilot, came out of the plane and helped with the bags. Five minutes later the plane began to taxi out to the runway.

"I imagine it won't be long before we all will have to process through a Customs checkpoint. This VIP treatment is getting looked at with a critical eye, especially among the younger officers," Rivers said.

"He felt put out?" Clint asked. He was sitting across the aisle from her. One comfortable seat lined each side of the aisle with six passenger seats in all. Deer sat in the seat behind him.

"Yes. There was a day where a junior officer would be thrilled to represent his boss and meet a so-called VIP. I think that day is over. That man was polite, but he obviously felt we were wasting his precious time."

"Did he give you any idea what big thing he thought he was missing out on?"

"No, but this time I didn't have to even fake not being interested. We already know," she said.

The plane took off and the flight to Guam for the most part was uneventful. The one surprise came a little more than two hours into the flight when Clint received a lengthy text from Buzz in Washington D.C.

"As expected police response to location you provided

resulted in discovery of lone dead assassin and two dead security guards. What was unexpected was the discovery of a second dead assassin at a different location in the city. Both were found on balconies high enough to provide line of sight to the US consulate. The president provided a short speech there this morning. Both had same type sniper rifle. Second assassin killed by Busan policeman whose connection to all this is under a lot of scrutiny. Needless to say, this has shaken the Secret Service and the South Koreans."

Clint read the text a second time before typing his reply.

"Interesting, definitely a lucky day for the good guys."

He considered adding to his return text that it was a lucky day for him, too, but he didn't. The thought made him realize that his near-death experience at the hands, or should he say legs of the North Korean, had shaken him a little more than he expected. He had been in numerous tight spots before, but this time it would take a while to shake the thought of the man's legs slowly choking the life out of him.

The copilot squeezed out of the cockpit and walked to the back of the plane nodding at Clint as he walked by. When he returned, he offered Clint a paper cup full of coffee.

"Thanks," Clint said.

"No problem, there's more in the pot back there. When they wake up let them know," he said and returned to the cockpit.

Clint took a couple of sips of coffee and placed the cup in the cup holder. Despite the caffeine, he was asleep in a few minutes.

"Don't you want to be awake for the landing? It's a beautiful view out the window," Rivers said while grasping his arm in her outstretched hand.

"Good morning," he mumbled and stretched. "Or afternoon."

He looked out his window and saw that the plane had started its descent. The island and ocean now shared the view out his window. He looked at his phone and saw another text. "Uber driver will meet you and Deer at airport to take you to doctor.

He will have sign saying CS Travel."

"At what hotel are we staying?" Clint asked Rivers.

She smiled at him. While he had said he would spend the few days in Guam with her, she still had had her doubts.

"The Outrigger. It's on the beach."

"Sure you can put up with me for the next day or so?"

"I'll try."

Eleanor Rivers wondered if Clint felt obligated to spend the time with her or if he actually wanted to. She could pose the question, but then that would be stupid. Besides, other than affecting her ego, why should she care? And, she did want him to stay.

"I'll need to get Sara to the clinic, but then I'll join you. Can you wait on dinner until I get there?"

"Of course, but don't be too late," Rivers said.

"I can find my own way to the doctor," Deer said, inserting herself into the conversation. "I'd hate to interrupt anything."

"Don't worry," Clint said. "Once you're in the doctor's good hands, I'll leave you to him. Besides, I don't want to be there when he yells at you for waiting so long."

"I feel a little better today. I think the antibiotics you found for me are starting to work. I think the scarring will be the worst part."

They parted company at the airport. The hotel had a car waiting for Rivers, and Clint found the Uber driver without difficulty. Barely a minute after the car left the airport, Deer's phone rang.

Clint could tell that the call had come from either Buzz or Dolly. After reassuring the caller that she was going to survive, Deer spent the majority of the time listening. The call ended at least five minutes before they were dropped off at the small, modern looking medical clinic, but the two finished the ride in silence.

After announcing their arrival to the receptionist, the two

were shown to a private waiting room.

"The call was mostly a recap of what's been happening," Deer said after double checking that they were alone. "There were few new items. First the security video coverage in the building you went to had been messed up. The Koreans will try to salvage it, but we'll see. Most of the intercepts and liaison reporting indicate there is considerable debate whether the cop who killed the second assassin is a hero or a traitor. A couple of our own senior civilians in government have been quietly arrested. Both our government and the Korean government are trying to keep a lid on all this, but as you can imagine the few leaks that have already made it out have created quite an interest in the press. And finally, the Korean security agencies have their hands full now that they have a good reason to believe that there are other North Koreans still in country around Busan."

"I'm just glad we're out of there. I would've liked to have spent a week or two being a tourist, but that will have to come later."

"This may be a silly question, but are you okay spending the next couple days with Eleanor?"

"It's probably just what I need at this point," Clint said. "I'll stay in touch, but once the doctor says you are going to be fine, I'll make reservations out of here.

As expected, the doctor expressed more than a little bit of frustration with Deer for waiting so long to see a doctor. He only took a few seconds to examine the wound before stating that fixing what had been ignored required surgery, a more focused treatment with antibiotics, and at least one or two follow up procedures.

"Absolutely no more wrapping tee shirts around the wound and wishing for the best," he said. "I'll have someone in here in a minute to take you to a room where you can get into a gown. Then we'll get to work."

The doctor left and Deer frowned. "I don't think this is going to be fun."

"Your punishment for dragging me into this," Clint said with a grin.

"Sorry about that. You might as well take off."

"Okay, I may swing by before I leave the island."

"Don't. I'll be fine. Have fun. Will you be heading straight home?"

"I'm thinking of going to Las Vegas. There's a buried treasure there I've been wanting to get back to."

Deer looked at him with raised eyebrows, but Clint didn't say anything more. He winked and walked away.

Title: *Dead Men Can Kill*™
- Author: Bob Doerr
- Publisher: TotalRecall Publications, Inc.
- Format: HARDCOVER, 6.14" x 9.21"
- 13-digit ISBN: 978-1-59095-758-5
- Paper Back: ISBN: 978-1-59095-759-2
- Book: ISBN: 978-1-59095-761-5
- Number of pages: 320
- Publication: December 8, 2009

When Jim West, a former Air Force Special Agent with the Office of Special Investigations, moves back to New Mexico, his goal is simple: start an easy going second career as a professional lecturer on investigative techniques to colleges and civic organizations. He never envisioned that his practical demonstration of forensic hypnosis on stage with a state university student would stir up memories of an 18-year old murder mystery. When the student is murdered three days later, West finds himself ensnared in a web of intrigue that pits him and the small town's authorities against a ruthless, psychotic killer.

An aggressive reporter for the town newspaper seeks out West for help with the story, but after one of her co-workers is murdered, she quickly aligns her efforts with West and the Sheriff. As West works closely with her, he begins to wonder if this could be the first real relationship for him since his devastating divorce a few years earlier.

The killer, though, has other plans for the reporter and the story takes fascinating twists and turns, leading to an inevitable, riveting confrontation.

Look out for a new hero on the mystery/thriller landscape! Jim West, retired military investigator, is resourceful, intuitive, pragmatic and always competent. All of West's abilities are tested when he matches wits with psychopathic serial killer William White, a man whose appreciation for murder is surpassed only by his delight in domination. Bob Doerr has crafted a must-read addition to the genre in Dead Men Can Kill, which evolves from absorbing story to absolute page-turner as West closes in on a killer who is supposedly dead. Highly recommended!

--Dallin Malmgren, author of...
The Whole Nine Yards   The Ninth Issue   Is This for a Grade?

A Jim West™ Mystery/Thriller

Title: *Cold Winter's Kill*™
- Author: Bob Doerr
- Publisher: TotalRecall Publications, Inc.
- Format: HARDCOVER, 6.14" x 9.21"
- 13-digit ISBN: 978-1-59095-762-2
- Paper Back: ISBN: 978-1-59095-763-9
- Book: ISBN: 978-1-59095-764-6
- Number of pages: 288
- Publication: Dec 8, 2009

Cold Winter's Kill is a fast-paced thriller that takes place in the scenic mountains of Lincoln County, New Mexico and throws Jim West into a race against time to stop a psychopath who abducts and kills a young blonde every Christmas...

It was one of those phone calls former Air Force Special Agent Jim West never wanted to receive--an old friend calling to ask if he could drive down to Ruidoso, New Mexico to help locate his daughter who has disappeared while on a ski trip with friends. Jim found himself heading to Ruidoso even though he believed, much like the local authorities, that if she had gone missing in the mountains in December, her survival chances were slim. He didn't want to be there when they found her, but still he drove on.

Once in Ruidoso, Jim discovers a sinister coincidence that changes everything. It appears that someone is abducting and killing one young blond every year around Christmas. The race is on--can Jim locate his friend's daughter in time? But why is this happening and who's doing it?

Jim can't wait for the local authorities to raise the priority of their search, or for the pending blizzard to pass. In his haste he puts himself in the killer's sights. Will he, too, suffer from a cold winter's kill?

"GREAT SUSPENSE! In *Cold Winter's Kill* Bob Doerr grabs your attention from the beginning and holds it until the last sentence. Hard to put down!"

> *--Shelba Nicholson*
> former Women's Editor, *Texarkana Gazette*

A Jim West™ Mystery/Thriller

Title: *Loose Ends Kill*™
- Author: Bob Doerr
- Publisher: TotalRecall Publications, Inc.
- Format: HARDCOVER, 6.14" x 9.21"
- 13-digit ISBN: 978-1-59095-717-2
- Paper Back: ISBN: 978-1-59095-718-9
- Book: ISBN: 978-1-59095-719-6
- Number of pages: 288
- Publication: Oct 27, 2010

LOOSE ENDS KILL **is a fast-paced mystery/thriller** that takes place in the historic city of San Antonio, Texas, and throws Jim West into the middle of a police investigation of the murder of an old friend's wife. The police already believe they have the killer in custody – West's friend.

West is drawn into this mystery by a call from the old friend who requests his assistance. West agrees to help his friend and digs deep to try to find another suspect. In the process he soon discovers that he is being followed and targeted for harassment, but by whom?

West quickly discovers that he didn't know his old friend's wife as well as he thought. To his surprise, he learns that she has had a number of affairs dating back for more than a decade. In fact, while investigating the murder, he realizes that his friend and he may be the only two people unaware of her philandering behavior.

Theorizing that one of her lovers could have had just as much motive as her husband, West starts turning over the rocks identifying one lover after another. In doing so, West unintentionally ignites an outbreak of more death and mayhem. The police and his friend's lawyers want West to go back home. The police even threaten to arrest him.

Soon, West believes the real killer wants him gone or dead. Deciding the only way to resolve the case before the outside pressures force him to leave, he sets a trap for the killer using himself as bait. However, he soon learns he may have only outsmarted himself.

A Jim West™ Mystery/Thriller

Title: *Another Colorado Kill*™
- Author: Bob Doerr
- Publisher: TotalRecall Publications, Inc.
- Format: HARDCOVER, 6.14" x 9.21"
- 13-digit ISBN: 978-1-59095-784-4
- Paper Back: ISBN: 978-1-59095-785-1
- Book: ISBN: 978-1-59095-786-8
- Number of pages: 288
- Publication Date: September 06, 2011

It was supposed to be a short, fun golf outing, but when Jim West and his friend Edward "Perry" Mason stumble across a dead body in a restroom at a rest stop along I-25, things turn bad and then only get worse.

With the golf outing shot, West intends to stay in Colorado Springs only for a day or two. However, when two more murder victims turn up – one with West's name handwritten in her notebook - the heat on West skyrockets. The police instruct him to stick around, and soon he discovers that while the police may want to pin the crimes on him, the killer wants him out of the picture. Way out – like dead.

West's only ally is Lieutenant Michelle Prado, a tall red head with large green eyes that captivate West. Assigned to keep an eye on West, Lieutenant Prado decides the best way to do so is to keep him close. West and Prado do their own digging into the investigation. In the process, Jim wonders how close their relationship will evolve.

It seems to West that as the police focus less on him, the killer intensifies his focus on him. Barely surviving an initial confrontation, West realizes he must take the initiative. If he doesn't, or perhaps even if he does - he may end up as just another Colorado kill.

A Jim West™ Mystery/Thriller

Title: *No One Else To Kill*™

- Author: Bob Doerr
- Publisher: TotalRecall Publications, Inc.
- Format: HARDCOVER, 6.14" x 9.21"
- 13-digit ISBN: 978-1-59095-422-5
- Paper Back: ISBN: 978-1-59095-423-2
- eBook: ISBN: 978-1-59095-424-9
- Number of pages in the finished book: 352
- Publication Date: December 4, 2012

No One Else to Kill, **Bob Doerr, TotalRecall Publications** - In this newest book in the popular Jim West series, Mr. West finds himself stood up and out of town. Looking forward to some R & R he keeps his reservation at the remote hunting lodge. Located in the Pecos Wilderness area in New Mexico it's a hunter's haven. Expecting to do nothing other than relax, he has no idea what the rest of the weekend holds for him. When a murder takes place, the hotel guest are detained and no one is beyond suspicion. The sheriff is called in, and while the investigation is underway, a second murder takes place. Both crimes are clearly related, but by whom and why? With time running out and unable to find a motive, the legal experts seek Jim's help.

2013
Eric Hoffer Award
WINNER
Excellence in
Independent
Publishing

2013
da Vinci Eye
FINALIST
Eric Hoffer Award
Excellence in
Independent Publishing

The cover for *No One Else To Kill* **is a 2013 finalist for the da Vinci Eye award.**

Bob's four previous novels in the series are titled *Dead Men Can Kill, Cold Winter's Kill, Loose Ends Kill,* and *Another Colorado Kill.* The latter two were selected as Eric Hoffer Award finalists for 2010 and 2011, respectively.

Bob Doerr's *No One Else To Kill* was awarded the Grand Prize in the "Books With Out Publishers" writing contest at www.ultimateherocontest.com

A Jim West™ Mystery/Thriller

Title: *Caffeine Can Kill*™
- Author: Bob Doerr
- Publisher: TotalRecall Publications, Inc.
- Hard Cover: ISBN: 978-1-59095-561-1
- Paper Back: ISBN: 978-1-59095-562-8
- eBook: ISBN: 978-1-59095-563-5
- Number of pages in the finished book: 240
- Publication Date: 2017

This Jim West mystery/thriller, the sixth in the series, finds Jim traveling to the Texas Hill Country to attend the grand opening of a friend's winery and vineyard. Upon arriving in Fredericksburg, Jim witnesses a brutal kidnapping at a local coffee shop. The next morning while driving down an unpaved country road to the grand opening, he comes across an active crime scene barely a quarter mile from his friend's winery. A Fredericksburg policeman who talked to Jim the day before at the kidnapping scene recognizes Jim and asks him to identify the body of a dead young woman as the woman who was kidnapped. Jim does, and as a result of this unwelcome relationship with the police is asked the next morning to identify the body of another murdered person as the man who had kidnapped the young woman. A third murder throws Jim's vacation into complete disarray and draws Jim and a female friend into the sights of one of the killers.

A Jim West™ Mystery/Thriller

Title: *Greed Can Kill*™
- Author: Bob Doerr
- Publisher: TotalRecall Publications, Inc.
- Hard Cover: ISBN: 978-1-59095-730-1
- Paper Back: ISBN: 978-1-59095-731-8
- eBook: ISBN: 978-1-59095-741-7
- Number of pages in the finished book: 280
- Publication Date: 2017

This adventure finds Jim traveling to Fabens, TX, in an effort to locate an old acquaintance who had written Jim a cryptic letter asking for his help in finding a briefcase. In Fabens, he discovers that someone has murdered his friend. Jim provides a copy of the letter to the local police explaining that he has no idea where the briefcase is or how to decipher the sets of numbers provided in the letter. Figuring there is nothing more he can do, Jim starts his trek back home. He plans to spend a night or two relaxing at the Lodge in Cloudcroft, NM, on his way only to find that he is being followed. An ominous, unidentified phone caller gives Jim an ultimatum - find the briefcase and turn it over to him within a week.

A violent confrontation in Cloudcroft verifies Jim's worst suspicion, a Mexican drug cartel wants the briefcase. The confrontation also brings the FBI into the picture. They also want Jim to continue his search. The search takes Jim to the New Mexican ghost town of Chloride where the final confrontation takes place and Jim finds out who the bad guys really are.

Author Bob Doerr Uses his special knowledge to provide authentic details in his novels about how law enforcement agencies do their work.

www.bobdoerr.com

A Jim West™ Mystery/Thriller

Title: *The Attack*™

- Author: Bob Doerr
- Publisher: TotalRecall Publications, Inc.
- Hard Cover ISBN: 978-1-59095-145-3
- Paper Back: ISBN: 978-1-59095-146-0
- Book: ISBN: 978-1-59095-147-7
- Number of pages in the finished book:
- Publication Date:

A terrorist team has just set off four explosive devices in an international airport close to New York City. The leader of the terrorists, Ahmad Khalin, survives the attack and plans to attack a second U.S. airport within the month. As Khalin makes his escape from the New York area he is involved in a shooting in Connecticut. Clint Smith, a U.S. government agent assigned to an ultra-secret agency, is at a restaurant across the street when the shooting occurs. He responds to the scene to see if he can help, but Khalin is gone. On a hunch, Teresa Deer, Smith's boss, sends Smith after Khalin. Smith's pursuit takes him to Bar Harbor, Maine; Wiesbaden, Germany; the Costa Brava, Spain; Northern Scotland; Lake of the Woods, Ontario, Canada; and finally into Saskatchewan, Canada, where the final confrontation takes place. Throughout the pursuit, a number of interesting characters add to the subplots and try to survive their involvement in the chase.

A Clint Smith Thriller™

Title: *The Group*™
- Author: Bob Doerr
- Publisher: TotalRecall Publications, Inc.
- Hard Cover ISBN: 978-1-59095-568-0
- Paper Back: ISBN: 978-1-59095-569-7
- eBook: ISBN: 978-1-59095-570-3
- Number of pages in the finished book: 288
- Publication Date: 2016

A fast-moving international thriller that pits a lone government operative, known as a hunter, against an unknown group of assassins who pose a worldwide threat.

Someone is killing off the world's rich and famous. The murders are sophisticated, requiring precision and skill. The international community is in an uproar but has no leads in its attempt to find the assassins. The victims were members of the Bilderberg Group, an international, loose knit group of the uber rich that meet annually. While the attacks have not had a direct impact on the U.S., Theresa Deer, Director of the Special Section, a small unit whose existence is known by only a handful in the U.S. government, sees this new age League of Assassins as a national threat. She sends her hunters out. Clint Smith finds their trail Switzerland where his discovery almost leads to his own death. The hunt leads him to Mallorca, Spain, where he witnesses a helicopter attack on a villa where a number of attendees from the Bilderberg conference were holding a follow-on meeting of their own. Smith picks up the trail a couple weeks later in Las Vegas, NV, and in his hunt finds out that he is no longer the hunter. He has become the prey.

A Clint Smith Thriller™

Title: *The assassins*™

- Author: Bob Doerr
- Publisher: TotalRecall Publications, Inc.
- Hard Cover ISBN: 9781590951958
- Paper Back: ISBN: 9781590951965
- eBook: ISBN: 9781590951972
- Number of pages in the finished book: 242
- Publication Date: 2018

A disputed election has divided the nation, and a handful of senior government officials have conspired to have the North Koreans assassinate the President of the United States. Believing the assassination attempt to be only days away, Theresa Deer, Director of the Special Section, a small unit whose existence is known by only a few in the U.S. government, is tasked to interdict the man intent on providing the North Koreans vital information about the president's itinerary for his visit to South Korea. While Deer succeeds in her mission, she is severely injured and finds herself being hunted by the North Korean assassins. Clint Smith is sent to Korea to help Deer get back to the U.S. and finds himself caught in a deadly game of cat and mouse with the North Koreans. With no one in the U.S. government to turn to for help, and the South Koreans now also hunting them, getting out of South Korea alive is looking unlikely.

A Clint Smith Thriller™

Title: *The Enchanted Coin*™
- Author: Bob Doerr
- Publisher: TotalRecall Publications, Inc.
- Hardcover, ISBN: 978-1-59095-083-8
- Paper Back: ISBN: 978-1-59095-084-5
- Book: ISBN: 978-1-59095-085-2
- Audio ISBN: 9781590952788
- Number of pages in the finished book: 130
- Publication Date: September 17, 2013

We have all heard of tales of UFO's, ghosts, people who say they can talk to the spirits, ancient curses, and magical talismans. Most of us automatically dismiss them as false, figments of people's imagination, and understandably so. However, might not just a few of them be true? I don't know, but I heard this story from a young man the other day who swore the fascinating tale I have set forth in this book really did really occur, because it happened to him. You be the judge.

Title: *The Rescue of Vincent*™
- Author: Bob Doerr
- Publisher: TotalRecall Publications, Inc.
- Paperback, ISBN: 978-1-59095-279-5
- eBook: ISBN: 978-1-59095-280-1
- Audio ISBN:
- Number of pages in the finished book: 160
- Publication Date: October 28, 2014

The Rescue of Vincent: Book 2 in The Enchanted Coin Series is a 31,000-word fantasy adventure targeted at Middle Grade readers. Imagine being a fourteen-year-old again and finding a coin that seems to give off a light of its own. The coin has your name on it, and instructs you to toss it into a fountain next to the Tree of Life. That's what happens in The Rescue of Vincent, and what starts my protagonist off on a magical adventure that many young boys and girls would love to have. This book is "G" rated.

Title: *The Magic of Vex*™
- Author: Bob Doerr
- Publisher: TotalRecall Publications, Inc.
- Paper Back: ISBN: 978-1-59095-309-9
- eBook: ISBN: 978-1-59095-280-1
- Audio ISBN: 978-1-59095-281-8
- Number of pages in the finished book: 140
- Publication Date: August 4, 2015

Samantha Gillespie's discovery of a magic coin results in her transportation to the strange world of Vex where magic is real and where she has to overcome a number of challenges if she ever hopes to return home.

What happened to Samantha was totally unexpected and quite frightening. It led her to an adventure that many might think impossible to believe, but it did.

You be the judge.

The Enchanted Coin Series

Locate Bob on Facebook and let him know how you like his books.

Author Bob Doerr Uses his special knowledge to
provide authentic details in his novels about how law
enforcement agencies do their work.
For a complete list of books by Bob Doerr,
a preview of upcoming titles and more
visit his website.
www.bobdoerr.com.

Titles by Bob Doerr

Mystery Detective Suspense Thrillers

Dead Men Can Kill

Cold Winters Kill

Another Colorado Kill

Loose Ends Kill

No One Else To Kill

Caffeine Can Kill

Greed Can Kill

Action Adventure Series

The Attack

The Group

The Assassins

Mouse Gate Series

The Enchanted Coin

The Rescue of Vincent

The Magic of Vex